U0037546

Ode to
A Nightingale
EX-LIBRIS
©DEE TEN PUBLISHING

夜鶯頌

濟慈詩選／

中・英對照雙語版

Ode to A Nightingale

約翰・濟慈——著

王明鳳————譯

笛藤出版

前　言

唯美詩化的文字，猶如夜幕蒼穹中的密佈星羅，自悠久的歷史長河之中散發出璀璨迷人的耀目光環，是人類精神世界中無價的瑰寶。千百年來，由各種文字所組成的篇章，經由傳遞淬煉，使其在各種文學彙集而成的花園中不斷綻放出絢幻之花，讓人們沉浸於美好的閱讀時光。

作者們以凝練的語言、鮮明的節奏，反映著世界萬象的生活樣貌，並以各種形式向世人展現他們內心豐富多彩的情感世界。每個民族、地域的文化都有其精妙之處，西洋文學往往直接抒發作者的思想，愛、自由、和平，言盡而意亦盡，毫無造作之感。

18 ～ 19 世紀，西洋文學的發展進入彰顯浪漫主義色彩的時期。所謂浪漫主義，就是用熱情奔放的言辭、絢麗多彩的想像與直白誇張的表現手法，直接抒發出作者對理想世界熱切追求與渴望的情感。《世界經典文學 中英對照》系列，精選了浪漫主義時期一些作者們的代表作，包括泰戈爾的《新月集》、《漂鳥集》；雪萊的《西風頌》；濟慈的《夜鶯頌》；拜倫的《漫步在美的光影》；葉慈的《塵世玫瑰》。讓喜文之人盡情地徜徉於優美的文字間，領略作者及作品的無盡風采，享受藝術與美的洗禮。本系列所精選出的作品在世界文學領域中皆為經典名作，因此特別附上英文，方便讀者對照賞析英文詩意之美，並可同時提升英文閱讀與寫作素養。

在這一系列叢書當中，有對自然的禮讚，有對愛與和平的歌頌，有對孩童時代的讚美，也有對人生哲理的警示。作者們在其一生中經歷了數次變革，以文字的形式寫下了無數天真、優美、現實、或悲哀的篇章，以無限的情懷吸引著所有各國藝文人士。文學界的名人郭沫若與冰心便是因受到了泰戈爾這位偉大的印度著名詩人所著詩歌的影響，在一段時期內寫出了很多類似的詩作。在世界文學界諸多名人當中有貴族、政治名人、社會名流、也有普羅大眾，他們來自不同的國家、種族，無論一生平順或是坎坷，但其所創作品無一不是充滿了對世間的熱愛，對未來美好世界的無限嚮往。

編按：由於經過時間變遷、地域上的區別，許多遣辭用句也多所改變，為期望能更貼近現代讀者，特將原譯文經過潤飾，希望讀者能以貼近生活的語詞，欣賞濟慈所欲傳達的詩意哲理。

目　錄

獻詩——致李・亨特先生／

榮譽和瑰麗早已逝去，

因為我們在清晨漫步之時，

已看不到繚繞的爐香

飄向東方，與微笑的白日相見；

也不見成群的少女呢喃細語，年輕又歡快，

提著裝有穀穗、

玫瑰、石竹、紫羅蘭的花籃，

在早春五月去祭拜花神弗羅拉的神龕。

但有流傳下來的詩歌為生活增添了樂趣；

我為自己的命運感到慶幸：

在這個時代，在舒爽的林蔭裡

即使沒有牧羊神，我也能感到

林木蓊鬱的美妙，我還能把

這貧乏的一切獻祭給您。

To Leigh Hunt, Esq.

Glory and loveliness have passed away;
For if we wander out in early morn,
No wreathed incense do we see upborne
Into the east, to meet the smiling day:
No crowd of nymphs soft-voiced and young, and gay,
In woven baskets bringing ears of corn,
Roses, and pinks, and violets, to adorn
The shrine of Flora in her early May.
But there are left delights as high as these,
And I shall ever bless my destiny,
That in a time, when under pleasant trees
Pan is no longer sought, I feel a free,
A leafy luxury, seeing I could please,
With these poor offerings, a man like thee.

致我的弟弟喬治／

今天我見到了許多奇景：
首先朝陽吻去了清晨
眼中的淚水；世間的詩人
憑倚在黃昏如羽毛般輕柔的金色光芒中；
浩瀚的海洋，碧綠幽藍，
那些船隻、奇岩、洞穴、希望和恐懼，
神祕的潮汐聲，凡聽到的人
必會思及未來，緬懷過往。
親愛的喬治啊！就在我寫信的當下，
月神辛西亞在她新婚的晚上，
透過絲幔羞怯地向外窺視，
流露出半掩的歡愉。
然而，若不是因為聯想到你，
這天空和海洋的奇觀又怎會呈現在我眼前？

To My Brother George

Many the wonders I this day have seen:
The sun, when first he kist away the tears
That fill'd the eyes of morn; – the laurell'd peers
Who from the feathery gold of evening lean; –
The ocean with its vastness, its blue green,
Its ships, its rocks, its caves, its hopes, its fears, –
Its voice mysterious, which whoso hears
Must think on what will be, and what has been.
E'en now, dear George, while this for you I write,
Cynthia is from her silken curtains peeping
So scantly, that it seems her bridal night,
And she her half-discover'd revels keeping.
But what, without the social thought of thee,
Would be the wonders of the sky and sea?

致——／

假如我有英俊的面孔，我的嘆息
就會輕快地飄進你如象牙白般的
貝耳，找到你溫柔的心；
激情將會圍繞著我，領我冒險：
可是啊，我不是殺敵的騎士，
沒有盔甲在我的胸前閃耀；
我也不是林中快樂的牧童，
雙唇因為少女的目光而微顫。
但我仍然溺愛著你——讚你甜蜜，
因為你比希布拉蜂蜜般的玫瑰還甜美，
當我浸潤在醉人的露水裡。
噢！我將品嚐那滴露珠，
當月亮露出她蒼白的臉龐時，
我要採集一些露水，用那些魔法和咒語。

To-

Had I a man's fair form, then might my sighs
Be echoed swiftly through that ivory shell
Thine ear, and find thy gentle heart; so well
Would passion arm me for the enterpris:
But ah! I am no knight whose foeman dies;
No cuirass glistens on my bosom's swell;
I am no happy shepherd of the dell
Whose lips have trembled with a maiden's eyes.
Yet must I dote upon thee, – call thee sweet,
Sweeter by far than Hybla's honey'd roses
When steep'd in dew rich to intoxication.
Ah! I will taste that dew, for me 'tis meet,
And when the moon her pallid face discloses,
I'll gather some by spells, and incantation.

寫給 G.A.W. ／

低頭側目微笑的少女啊！

在一天中的哪個神聖時刻

你最為迷人？是你迷失沉醉

在甜美話語中的時候？

或是你拿著枝葉編織的花環

靜靜思考的時候？或是隨意披著長袍

突然跑去擁抱朝陽之際，

或是左閃右避地跑跳，小心翼翼不踩到花朵的時候？

也許是當你微張著紅寶石般的唇

凝神傾聽的時分。

但你被上天孕育得如此完美，

我永遠說不出你哪種情致最好：

就像很難說哪位優雅女神

在阿波羅面前舞得最美。

To G.A.W.

Nymph of the downward smile, and sidelong glance,
In what diviner moments of the day
Art thou most lovely? When gone far astray
Into the labyrinths of sweet utterance?
Or when serenely wand'ring in a trance
Of sober thought? Or when starting away,
With careless robe, to meet the morning ray,
Thou spar'st the flowers in thy mazy dance?
Haply 'tis when thy ruby lips part sweetly,
And so remain, because thou listenest:
But thou to please wert nurtured so completely
That I can never tell what mood is best.
I shall as soon pronounce which grace more neatly
Trips it before Apollo than the rest.

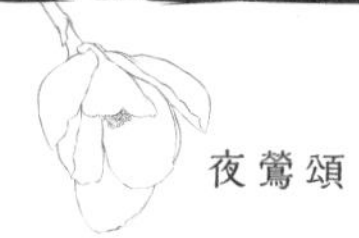

哦，孤獨！如果我必須和你共處／

哦，孤獨！如果我必須和你共處，
但願不是在這紛亂層疊的
灰暗建築裡，請與我一同攀上峭壁——
踏在大自然的瞭望臺上——看那裡的谷地、
花團錦簇的山坡、晶瑩剔透的河水，
看似近在咫尺；讓我守護著你
在林蔭下，看麋鹿的跳躍，
驚嚇到毛地黃花苞裡的蜜蜂。
儘管我願意和你觀賞這些景物，
但我更樂於和純潔的心靈親切交談；
傾聽精妙思想中的意象及語言，
這是我心靈的快樂；我相信
這必定是人類最高的樂趣，
兩個投緣者的共棲之地。

O Solitude! if I Must with Thee Dwell

O Solitude! if I must with thee dwell,
Let it not be among the jumbled heap
Of murky buildings; climb with me the steep, –
Nature's observatory – whence the dell,
Its flowery slopes, its river's crystal swell,
May seem a span; let me thy vigils keep
'Mongst boughs pavillion'd, where the deer's swift leap
Startles the wild bee from the fox-glove bell.
But though I'll gladly trace these scenes with thee,
Yet the sweet converse of an innocent mind,
Whose words are images of thoughts refin'd,
Is my soul's pleasure; and it sure must be
Almost the highest bliss of human-kind,
When to thy haunts two kindred spirits flee.

陣陣寒風從四面八方襲來／

陣陣寒風從四面八方襲來，
樹上的葉子已凋零過半；
夜空的星斗看起來如此冷酷，
而我還有很長的路要走；
然而，我感受不到嚴寒的空氣，
也沒聽到枯葉蕭颯，
或是穹廬中銀燈閃閃，
還有回家的漫漫長途；
因為我心中充滿了深厚情誼，
是我由小村舍中覓得，我看到
金髮的密爾頓內心充滿了憂鬱，
他對路希德的衷情已然陷溺；
可愛的蘿拉身著淺綠的衣裙，
忠實的彼得拉克頭戴光榮的桂冠。

Keen, Fitful Gusts Are Whisp'ring Here and There

Keen, fitful gusts are whisp'ring here and there
Among the bushes half leafless, and dry;
The stars look very cold about the sky,
And I have many miles on foot to fare.
Yet feel I little of the cool bleak air,
Or of the dead leaves rustling drearily,
Or of those silver lamps that burn on high,
Or of the distance from home's pleasant lair:
For I am brimfull of the friendliness
That in a little cottage I have found;
Of fair-hair'd Milton's eloquent distress,
And all his love for gentle Lycid drown'd;
Of lovely Laura in her light green dress,
And faithful Petrarch gloriously crown'd.

久居城市的人 ／

對一個久居城市的人來說，
能見到天空明朗的模樣，
能在蔚藍蒼穹的微笑下面
低聲禱告，是多麼逍遙！
能快樂地、慵懶地躺在
波浪般的青草間，展開一卷
親切動人，描繪愛與痛苦的小說品味，
還有什麼比這更愜意的呢？
遲暮歸家，聆聽著
夜鶯的啁啾，注視著
絢爛的浮雲從天際飄過，
他哀嘆白天竟如此短暫，
猶如天使的淚滴滑落在
透明的空氣中，悄然不見。

To One Who Has Been Long in City Pent

To one who has been long in city pent,
'Tis very sweet to look into the fair
And open face of heaven, – to breathe a prayer
Full in the smile of the blue firmament.
Who is more happy, when, with hearts content,
Fatigued he sinks into some pleasant lair
Of wavy grass, and reads a debonair
And gentle tale of love and languishment?
Returning home at evening, with an ear
Catching the notes of Philomel, – an eye
Watching the sailing cloudlet's bright career,
He mourns that day so soon has glided by:
E'en like the passage of an angel's tear
That falls through the clear ether silently.

清晨別友／

給我一枝金筆，讓我倚靠著
花叢，在清淨高遠的境地；
給我一張比星光更瑩白的便箋，
不然就給我那位唱歌天使的玉手，
來撥動豎琴的銀弦：
讓綴滿珍珠的馬車、
粉紅的長袍、飄動的捲髮、鑲鑽的花瓶、
半張的翅膀和熱切的雙眸，自由滑翔。
讓悠揚的仙樂在我的耳際繚繞，
當美妙的樂曲悠然告終時，
讓我寫下一行瑰麗的曲調，
描繪九霄之上的種種美妙：
我的思想正在攀登高峰！
他不甘這麼快就忍受孤獨。

On Leaving Some Friends at an Early Hour

Give me a golden pen, and let me lean
On heap'd up flowers, in regions clear, and far;
Bring me a tablet whiter than a star,
Or hand of hymning angel, when 'tis seen
The silver strings of heavenly harp atween:
And let there glide by many a pearly car,
Pink robes, and wavy hair, and diamond jar,
And half discovered wings, and glances keen.
The while let music wander round my ears,
And as it reaches each delicious ending,
Let me write down a line of glorious tone,
And full of many wonders of the spheres:
For what a height my spirit is contending!
Tis not content so soon to be alone.

致拜倫／

拜倫！你那甜美的歌聲裡帶著憂傷，
讓人心裡感到柔情，
彷彿是悲憫之神曾低彈魯特琴，
而你，便把那悲傷的音調銘記於心，
使它得以流傳，卻沒有因而受苦而逝。
幽暗的悲傷並沒有使你的快樂減少：
你讓自己的悲傷
戴上了光暈，使它燦爛奪目；
當雲霧遮住金黃的月色，
月亮的邊緣仍閃爍著耀眼的輝煌，
琥珀的光輝從黑暗下透出，
又似烏雲石上美麗的紋路
垂死的天鵝，仍然發出顫音，唱著故事——
讓令人神往的故事——充滿著悅人的悲傷。

To Lord Byron

Byron, how sweetly sad the melody,
Attuning still the soul to tenderness,
As if soft Pity with unusual stress
Had touch'd her plaintive lute, and thou, being by,
Hadst caught the tones, nor suffer'd them to die.
O'ershadowing sorrow doth not make thee less
Delightful: thou thy griefs dost dress
With a bright halo, shining beamily;
As when a cloud a golden moon doth veil,
Its sides are ting'd with a resplendent glow,
Through the dark robe oft amber rays prevail,
And like fair veins in sable marble flow.
Still warble, dying swan, – still the tale,
The enchanting tale – the tale of pleasing woe.

噢！我愛晴朗夏日的黃昏／

噢！我愛晴朗夏日的黃昏。
當萬丈金光灑落西方，
銀白雲朵在輕柔的風中安靜地休憩，
我將一切拋得遠遠的、遠遠的，
拋棄卑微的思想，
暫緩小小的憂慮，去找尋，輕鬆地追尋
野外的芬芳、秀麗的自然，
撒個小謊讓內心擁有快樂。
用往昔的愛國事蹟，溫暖心房，
冥想密爾頓的命運——錫德尼的靈柩，——
讓他們剛正的形象在心中升起。
也許能借助詩歌的翅膀，翱翔天際，
在悠揚的悲傷遮住我雙眼的時候，
我會淌下溫馨的淚水。

Oh! How I Love, on a Fair Summer's Eve

Oh! how I love, on a fair summer's eve,
When streams of light pour down the golden west,
And on the balmy zephyrs tranquil rest
The silver clouds, – far, far away to leave
All meaner thoughts, and take a sweet reprieve
From little cares; to find, with easy quest,
A fragrant wild, with Nature's beauty drest,
And there into delight my soul deceive.
There warm my breast with patriotic lore,
Musing on Milton's fate – on Sydney's bier –
Till their stern forms before my mind arise:
Perhaps on the wing of Poesy upsoar, –
Full often dropping a delicious tear,
When some melodious sorrow spells mine eyes.

黑色的霧靄不再籠罩平原／

黑色的霧靄不再籠罩著平原，
經過了漫長陰鬱的一季，
和煦的天氣從南方誕生，
洗淨病懨懨天空中不當的污痕。
焦慮的時光中，痛苦終於解除，
得以享受久失的權利，感受五月的風光，
眼瞼上還有即將逝去的涼意，
如同夏日的雨滴在玫瑰葉上。
寧靜的思緒湧上心頭，如同
萌芽的嫩葉、悄然成熟的果實、秋日陽光
對著黃昏裡的稻穀默默微笑，
莎孚甜美的雙頰、嬰兒熟睡時的呼吸聲、
沙漏中慢慢流下的沙粒、
林中的小溪——一位詩人的死亡。

After Dark Vapours Have Oppressed Our Plains

After dark vapours have oppress'd our plains
For a long dreary season, comes a day
Born of the gentle South, and clears away
From the sick heavens all unseemly stains.
The anxious month, relieved from its pains,
Takes as a long–lost right, the feel of May,
The eyelids with the passing coolness play,
Like rose leaves with the drip of summer rains.
And calmest thoughts come round us – as of leaves
Budding – fruit ripening in stillness – autumn suns
Smiling at eve upon the qui et sheaves,–
Sweet Sappho's cheek, – a sleeping infant's breath –
The gradual sand that through an hour-glass runs, –
A woodland rivulet, – a Poet's death.

這動聽的故事如同一座小叢林——
寫於喬叟《花與葉故事》後／

這動聽的故事如同一座小叢林：

蜂蜜般甜美的詩句纏繞交織，滿是新意，

讓讀者在這境界中流連忘返，

走走停停，心中滿是甜蜜；

晶瑩的露珠往往不經意地

落在臉上，倍感清涼，

聽著鳥兒婉轉的歌聲，可以

探尋細腳紅雀跳往的幽徑。

噢！潔白的單純竟有如此魅力！

文雅的故事又是多麼動人心弦！

儘管我長久以來渴望榮譽，

此刻卻滿足於

躺在草地上，就像無人理會的啜泣者，

除了知更鳥默默地為他們悲傷。

This Pleasant Tale Is Like a Little Copse-

Written On A Blank Space At The End Of Chaucer's Tale Of The Flowre And The Lefe

This pleasant tale is like a little copse:
The honied lines so freshly interlace,
To keep the reader in so sweet a place,
So that he here and there full-heart'd stops;
And oftentimes he feels the dewy drops
Come cool and suddenly against his face,
And, by the wandering melody may trace
Which way the tender-legged linnet hops.
Oh! what a power has white Simplicity!
What mighty power has this gentle story!
I, that do ever feel athirst for glory,
Could at this moment be content to lie
Meekly upon the grass, as those whose sobbings
Were heard of none beside the mournful robins.

海頌／

在荒涼的岸邊，大海永遠在
喃喃低語，猛漲的潮水，
淹沒了萬千的岩洞，
直到赫卡蒂女神的咒語再次回歸沉靜；
此時你會見到大海的溫柔，
曾被波濤捲來的細小貝殼
會一動也不動地在你的腳邊數日，
最終擺脫了天上的風帶來的束縛。
啊！如果你的眼睛感覺迷惑疲累，
那就讓眼睛享受廣闊無邊的大海，
啊！如果你的耳朵被喧囂所擾，
或是厭倦了演奏的靡靡之音，
那就在古老的洞穴旁獨坐，靜靜冥想，
直到你驚醒，彷彿聽見海中仙女的悠揚歌聲！

On the Sea

It keeps eternal whisperings around
Desolate shores, and with its mighty swell
Gluts twice ten thousand caverns, till the spell
Of Hecate leaves them their old shadowy sound.
Often 'tis in such gentle temper found,
That scarcely will the very smallest shell
Be moved for days from where it sometime fell.
When last the winds of Heaven were unbound.
Oh ye! who have your eye-balls vexed and tired,
Feast them upon the wideness of the Sea;
Oh ye! whose ears are dinn'd with uproar rude,
Or fed too much with cloying melody, –
Sit ye near some old Cavern's Mouth and brood,
Until ye start, as if the sea-nymphs quired!

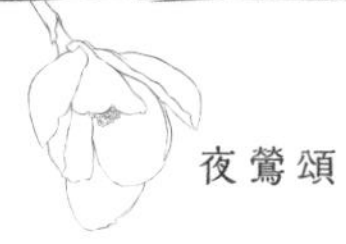

每當我害怕／

每當我害怕，生命也許會消逝，
來不及讓我用筆記下腦中活躍的思緒，
在堆積如山的書堆前，文字猶如
富饒的糧倉般收藏著豐碩的稻穀；
當我抬頭看著夜晚的星辰，
巨大的雲朵宛如浪漫故事的象徵，
我想我也許永遠活不到那時候，
無法以偶然的魔法之手描繪它們的影像；
每當我感覺，時間分秒流逝，
我將永遠見不到你，
永遠不能陶醉於不計後果的愛情，
更不能徜徉在愛的魔法仙境！——在廣闊的世界中，
我獨自站立在邊境思考
直到愛情和名譽都陷入虛無。

When I Have Fears That I May Cease to Be

When I have fears that I may cease to be
Before my pen has glean'd my teeming brain,
Before high piled books, in charact'ry,
Hold like rich garners the full-ripen'd grain;
When I behold, upon the night's starr'd face,
Huge cloudy symbols of a high romance,
And think that I may never live to trace
Their shadows, with the magic hand of chance;
And when I feel, fair creature of an hour!
That I shall never look upon thee more,
Never have relish in the faery power
Of unreflecting love! – then on the shore
Of the wide world I stand alone, and think
Till Love and Fame to nothingness do sink.

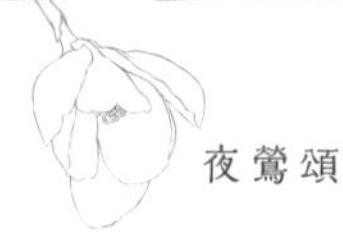

致尼羅河／

古老非洲的月山之子，
掌管著金字塔和鱷魚，
我們都說你富饒，而同時
我們的內心又浮現出一片沙漠。
從世界伊始，你孕育了眾多黑暗國度，
你是否真為一片沃土？或者，你欺瞞
這些在疲憊的勞作後崇敬你的人們，
他們還在開羅和德查尼兩地尋求歇息空間？
哦！希望這愚昧的想像是錯的！他們肯定
不會無知到認為自己以外的種種
都是荒涼貧瘠。你一定能像我們的河般
潤澤青草，你一定被晨曦的光芒
所照耀，你一定也擁有綠色的小島，
能快樂地向大海奔去。

To the Nile

Son of the old Moon-mountains African!
Chief of the Pyramid and Crocodile!
We call thee frui tful, and that very while,
A desert fills our seeing's inward span,
Nurse of swart nations since the world began,
Art thou so fruitful? or dost thou beguile
Such men to honour thee, who, worn with toil,
Rest for a space 'twixt Cairo and Decan?
O may dark fancies err! they surely do;
'Tis ignorance that makes a barren waste
Of all beyond itself. Thou dost bedew
Green rushes like our rivers, and dost taste
The pleasant sun-rise. Green isles hast thou too,
And to the sea as happily dost haste.

寫給 J.R. ／

如果一週能變永久，那我們

每週都會感覺到分別和溫暖的再會，

短短的一年變成了一千年，

臉頰上就會永遠閃耀著情誼；

我們能在狹小的空間裡久居，

時間變得無關緊要，

一天的旅程，變得漫長而緩慢，

讓我們在朦朧中忘記苦惱。

讓每個星期一都來自印度！

每個星期二來自富饒的地中海！

在那短短的一瞬，就有樂趣無窮，

讓我們的心靈永恆地跳躍！

今天早晨——我的朋友——甚至是昨日傍晚，教會我

怎樣珍惜這快樂的思緒。

To J.R.

O that a week could be an age, and we
Felt parting and warm meeting every week,
Then one poor year a thousand years would be,
The flush of welcome ever on the cheek:
So could we live long life in little space,
So time itself would be annihilate,
So a day's journey, in oblivious haze
To serve our joys would lengthen and dilate.
O to arrive each Monday morn from Ind!
To land each Tuesday from the rich Levant!
In little time a host of joys to bind,
And keep our souls in one eternal pant!
This morn, my friend, and yester-evening taught
Me how to harbour such a happy thought.

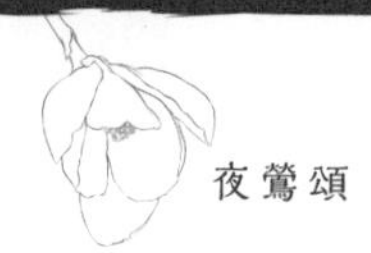

人生四季／

四季更迭構成了一年，

人的心靈也包含四季，

在朝氣蓬勃的春天，清晰的幻想，

瞬間帶來一切美景；

在奢華繁茂的夏天，

他反覆品味美好的春季思緒，

使自己沉湎其中，直到

靈魂消逝，思緒真正成為自我的一部分。

在秋日的港灣中，

他得以安歇，當他收起了疲累的翅膀，

滿足於眼前慵懶的霧色，讓美景

如門前的溪流，靜靜流淌。

他也有冬天，蒼白而醜陋，

否則他會遺忘凡人的本性。

Four Seasons Fill the Measure of the Year

Four seasons fill the measure of the year;
Four seasons are there in the mind of man.
He hath his lusty spring, when fancy clear
Takes in all beauty with an easy span;
He hath his summer, when luxuriously
He chews the honied cud of fair spring thoughts,
Till, in his soul dissolv'd, they come to be
Part of himself. He hath his autumn ports
And havens of repose, when his tired wings
Are folded up, and he content to look
On mists in idleness; to let fair things
Pass by unheeded as a threshold brook.
He hath his winter too of pale misfeature,
Or else he would forget his mortal nature.

致艾爾薩巨岩／

聽著，陡峭如海上金字塔的巨岩，
用海鷗的叫聲給我答案吧！
你的雙肩何時披上了巨流？
你的額頭何時受到陽光遮蔽？
造物主何時命你脫離海底夢境，
輕快地將睡夢中的你
舉到雷電和光芒的懷裡，
還以潔白的雲朵覆蓋著你？
你不回答，因為你在熟睡。
你的生命有兩個永恆的沉默——
後者在空中，前者在深海裡；
首先是有鯨魚為伴的深海中，
另一個在雄鷹飛翔的空中。
只有地震才能讓你高聳於海面，
否則誰都不能將你巨大的身軀喚醒！

To Ailsa Rock

Hearken, thou craggy ocean pyramid!
Give answer from thy voice, – the sea-fowls' screams
When were thy shoulders mantled in huge streams?
When from the sun was thy broad forehead hid?
How long is't since the mighty Power bid
Thee heave to airy sleep from fathom dreams –
Sleep in the lap of thunder or sunbeams,
Or when grey clouds are thy cold coverlid?
Thou answer'st not, for thou art dead asleep;
Thy life is but two dead eternities –
The last i n air, the former i n the deep;
First with the whales, last in the eagle-skies
Drown'd wast thou till an earthquake made thee steep,
Another cannot wake thy giant size!

詠睡眠／

啊，靜謐午夜的溫柔安慰者，
你用善良的手指輕輕闔上
性喜幽暗的眼睛，讓它避開光芒，
進入神聖的遺忘之鄉；
啊，甜美的睡眠！如果這能讓你感到喜悅，
在讚美詩歌期間，就闔上我的雙眼。
或者等到「阿門」之後，再將罌粟
灑在我的床邊，帶來舒緩與慈愛；
拯救我吧，否則逝去的白晝將
照耀在枕頭上，徒增許多愁緒；
請幫我擺脫這好奇之心吧，
它會像鼴鼠一樣挖洞鑽進黑暗；
請把鑰匙鎖進上了油的鎖孔裡，
將我靈魂所在的寂靜棺木予以封存。

Sonnet to Sleep

O soft embalmer of the still midnight,
Shutting with careful fingers and benign
Our gloom-pleas'd eyes, embower'd from the light,
Enshaded in forgetfulness divine;
O soothest Sleep! if so it please thee, close,
In midst of this thine hymn, my willing eyes,
Or wait the Amen ere thy poppy throws
Around my bed its lulling charities;
Then save me, or the passed day will shine
Upon my pillow, breeding many woes:
Save me from curious conscience, that still hoards
Its strength for darkness, burrowing like a mole;
Turn the key deftly in the oiled wards,
And seal the hushed casket of my soul.

白日已盡，而甜蜜亦逝／

白日已盡，而甜蜜亦逝！
悅耳嗓音、甜美蜜唇、纖纖玉手、柔軟酥胸、
熱情的呼吸、輕柔的低語、溫軟耳語、
明亮的雙眸，豐盈的體態，細柔的腰肢！
嬌艷花朵和含苞待放的蓓蕾，在你面前相形失色，
我眼中所有的美景，都為之褪色，
我手中環抱過的種種，都不及你的美好，
所有的聲音、溫暖、聖潔、甚至是天堂——
都顯得不合時宜，在黃昏時消逝了，
在節日的薄暮，或香氣四溢的夜晚，
隱蔽的愛情開始編織幽黑的夜幕，隱藏喜悅；
但是，我今天已經閱讀過愛情的聖書，
上帝看到了我的齋戒和祈禱，會讓我安睡。

The Day Is Gone, and all Its Sweets Are Gone

The day is gone, and all its sweets are gone!

Sweet voice, sweet lips, soft hand, and softer breast,

Warm breath, light whisper, tender semi-tone,

Bright eyes, accomplished shape, and lang'rous waist!

Faded the flower and all its budded charms,

Faded the sight of beauty from my eyes,

Faded the shape of beauty from my arms,

Faded the voice, warmth, whiteness, paradise –

Vanished unseasonably at shut of eve,

When the dusk holiday – or holinight

Of fragrant-curtained love begins to weave

The woof of darkness thick, for hid delight;

But, as I've read love's missal through today,

He'll let me sleep, seeing I fast and pray.

我渴求你的仁慈／

我渴求你的仁慈、憐憫和愛情！是的，愛情！
我渴求仁慈、沒有欺騙的愛情；
專一、堅貞、絕無欺瞞，
開誠布公，潔白無瑕的愛！
哦，讓我完全地擁有你，完全——完全地屬於我！
你的姿態、美好、甜蜜熱烈的
愛情、你的吻，那雙手、靈動的眼睛，
溫暖、潔白、透明、風情萬種的酥胸，
全部的你——你的靈魂——請憐憫我，全都給我，
不要有任何保留，否則我會死去，
即使活著，也成為你卑微的奴隸，
被遺忘在悲苦的迷霧中，
生命的目的——我心中的樂趣
和雄心壯志將隱蔽，將如風一般飄逝。

I Cry Your Mercy

I cry your mercy – pity – love! – aye, love!
Merciful love that tantalizes not,
One-thoughted, never-wandering, guileless love,
Unmask'd, and being seen – without a blot!
O!let me have thee whole, – all – all – be mine!
That shape, that fairness, that sweet minor zest
Of love, your kiss, – those hands, those eyes divine,
That warm, white, lucent, million-pleasured breast, –
Yourself – your soul – in pity give me all,
Withhold no atom's atom or I die,
Or living on perhaps, your wretched thrall,
Forget, in the midst of idle misery,
Life's purposes, – the palate of my mind
Losing its gust, and my ambition blind!

夜鶯頌／

我心疼痛，困倦和麻木，

我的感官如同飲盡毒汁，

又有如吞下了鴉片，

很快地向忘川的河床沉去；

我並不是嫉妒你的好運，

而是為你的快樂感到高興——

你啊，林中的精靈，

在蓊鬱的山毛櫸的樹蔭下，

放聲高歌，用悠揚的音樂

盡情地歌頌夏天。

Ode to a Nightingale

My heart aches, and a drowsy numbness pains
My sense, as though of hemlock I had drunk,
Or emptied some dull opiate to the drains
One minute past, and Lethe-wards had sunk:
'Tis not through envy of thy happy lot,
But being too happy in thine happiness, –
That thou, light-winged Dryad of the trees,
In some melodious plot
Of beechen green, and shadows numberless,
Singest of summer in full-throated ease.

哦，來喝一口美酒吧！這佳釀
在地下深藏多年，
嚐起來令人想起花神和鄉間田野，
舞蹈、普羅旺斯的歌曲，和似火的驕陽！
哦，來一杯帶有南方溫暖的美酒，
滿溢真切、讓雙頰緋紅的靈感之泉，
杯緣上還閃動著珍珠般的泡沫，
嘴唇也被染上一抹紫色；
我要暢飲，遠離塵囂，
和你一起隱沒在幽深的林間。

O, for a draught of vintage! that hath been
Cool'd a long age in the deep-delved earth,
Tasting of Flora and the country green,
Dance, and Provençal song, and sunburnt mirth!
O for a beaker full of the warm South,
Full of the true, the blushful Hippocrene,
With beaded bubbles winking at the brim,
And purple-stained mouth;
That I might drink, and leave the world unseen,
And with thee fade away into the forest dim,

走得遠遠，全然忘懷

你所不知的綠葉間的一切，

忘記疲乏、熱病和煩躁，

這個人們對坐哀嘆的世界；

沼澤抖落些許悲傷將盡的灰髮，

韶華漸漸蒼白、瘦谷嶙峋，直至死亡；

思考會帶來無盡悲傷，

沉悶的眼中剩下絕望；

美麗無法讓眼眸閃亮，

新的戀情轉瞬就變得憔悴。

Fade far away, dissolve, and quite forget
What thou among the leaves hast never known,
The weariness, the fever, and the fret
Here, where men sit and hear each other groan;
Where palsy shakes a few, sad, last gray hairs,
Where youth grows pale, and spectre-thin, and dies;
Where but to think is to be full of sorrow
And leaden-eyed despairs,
Where Beauty cannot keep her lustrous eyes,
Or new Love pine at them beyond to-morrow.

走吧！走吧！我要向你飛去，

我不要乘坐酒神之豹駕馭的輪車，

而是要乘著詩歌的雙翼，將一切盡覽無遺，

儘管頭腦已感困頓疲乏；

我已經和你同行！夜晚這樣的恬靜，

月亮之后登上了寶座，

星星仙子們簇擁著她；

但是這裡卻是幽暗無光，

當微風拂過那朦朧的綠色和滿佈苔蘚的蜿蜒小徑，

才能留住天庭的一絲光線。

Away! away! for I will fly to thee,
Not charioted by Bacchus and his pards,
But on the viewless wings of Poesy,
Though the dull brain perplexes and retards:
Already with thee! tender is the night,
And haply the Queen-Moon is on her throne,
Cluster'd around by all her starry Fays;
But here there is no light,
Save what from heaven is with the breezes blown
Through verdurous glooms and winding mossy ways.

我看不清腳邊是何種花草，

也看不清掛在枝頭的是哪種芳香的花朵；

黑暗鋪天蓋地，只能猜想

是哪種當季花卉散發幽香，

在這草地、樹叢和野果樹旁；

白色的山楂花，田野中的薔薇；

藏在綠葉中易枯的紫羅蘭，

還有五月中旬的寵兒，

這盛滿朝露之酒的麝香薔薇，

在夏夜中與蟲聲唧唧為伴。

I cannot see what flowers are at my feet,
Nor what soft incense hangs upon the boughs,
But, in embalmed darkness, guess each sweet
Wherewith the seasonable month endows
The grass, the thicket, and the fruit-tree wild;
White hawthorn, and the pastoral eglantine;
Fast fading violets cover'd up in leaves;
And mid-May's eldest child,
The coming musk-rose, full of dewy wine,
The murmurous haunt of flies on summer eves.

我在黑暗中傾聽著，有許多次
我幾乎要愛上死亡的舒坦，
我窮盡詩句，呼喚他的名字，
請他將我微弱的氣息帶走，
此刻死亡看似無比豐盈：
在午夜安詳辭世，毫無痛苦，
當你的靈魂傾訴之際，
竟是這樣的陶醉神往！
你依舊歌唱著，而我再也聽不到——
那高昂的輓歌化為一抔泥土。

Darkling I listen; and, for many a time
I have been half in love with easeful Death,
Call'd him soft names in many a mused rhyme,
To take into the air my quiet breath;
Now more than ever seems it rich to die,
To cease upon the midnight with no pain,
While thou art pouring forth thy soul abroad
In such an ecstasy!
Still wouldst thou sing, and I have ears in vain –
To thy high requiem become a sod.

不死鳥啊，你會永生不息！

你不屈從於饑餓的年歲；

今夜，我聽見了你的歌聲，

古代的帝王和農夫也曾聽見，

也許，你的歌聲也曾激盪

露絲憂鬱的心，使她潸然淚下，

在異邦的田園裡，思念著家鄉；

這歌聲還常常使得

仙女打開充滿魔力的窗扉，在孤寂的仙境

望向咆哮兇險的大海。

Thou wast not born for death, immortal Bird!
No hungry generations tread thee down;
The voice I hear this passing night was heard
In ancient days by emperor and clown:
Perhaps the self-same song that found a path
Through the sad heart of Ruth, when, sick for home,
She stood in tears amid the alien corn;
The same that oft-times hath
Charm'd magic casements, opening on the foam
Of perilous seas, in faery lands forlorn.

孤寂！這個詞就像鐘聲，
提醒我離開你，回到孤身一人！
別了！幻象，你騙不了我，
欺騙的精靈，惡名昭彰。
別了！別了！你那哀怨的歌聲
已經穿越了草地，繞過了潺潺的溪流，
飄上山頂，漸漸遠去了；深埋在
附近林中的幽谷間：
這是幻覺，還是夢寐？
歌聲漸遠——我醒了，還是在睡夢中？

Forlorn! the very word is like a bell
To toll me back from thee to my sole self!
Adieu! the fancy cannot cheat so well
As she is fam'd to do, deceiving elf.
Adieu! adieu! thy plaintive anthem fades
Past the near meadows, over the still stream,
Up the hill-side; and now 'tis buried deep
In the next valley-glades:
Was it a vision, or a waking dream?
Fled is that music: – Do I wake or sleep?

希臘古甕頌／

你，寂靜的新娘，仍然保持童貞，
你，由沉默和漫長領養的孩童，
林中的史學家，竟能講述
這樣一個如花般美麗的故事，比詩句還瑰麗：
你以綠葉鑲邊、圍繞著傳說的形體，
是否講述神祇、人類，或者兩者
居住在坦蓓谷或阿卡迪谷的事蹟？
是哪樣的神祇或人類？少女是怎樣地不願意？
是哪樣熾熱的追求？少女又怎樣掙扎脫逃？
是那樣的風笛和鼓？是怎樣的狂喜？

Ode on a Grecian Urn

Thou still unravish'd bride of quietness,
Thou foster-child of silence and slow time,
Sylvan historian, who canst thus express
A flowery tale more sweetly than our rhyme:
What leaf-fring'd legend haunts about thy shape
Of deities or mortals, or of both,
In Tempe or the dales of Arcady?
What men or gods are these? What maidens loth?
What mad pursuit? What struggle to escape?
What pipes and timbrels? What wild ecstasy?

聽見音樂固然美妙，但那些聽不到的
卻更甜美；因此，溫柔的風笛，請繼續演奏：
不是為感官的耳朵而奏，而是更受喜愛，
為心靈演奏無聲的樂曲；
樹蔭下的俊朗少年啊，你不會停止
歌唱，樹木也不會枯萎凋零；
莽撞的情郎，你絕不、絕不會得到那個吻，
雖然你幾乎已經勝券在握——但是，請不要悲傷；
她不會衰老，即使你不能如願，
你仍會繼續愛著她，而她也將青春永駐！

Heard melodies are sweet, but those unheard
Are sweeter; therefore, ye soft pipes, play on;
Not to the sensual ear, but, more endear'd,
Pipe to the spirit ditties of no tone:
Fair youth, beneath the trees, thou canst not leave
Thy song, nor ever can those trees be bare;
Bold Lover, never, never canst thou kiss,
Though winning near the goal – yet, do not grieve;
She cannot fade, though thou hast not thy bliss,
For ever wilt thou love, and she be fair!

啊，幸福、幸福的枝枒！你那樹葉
永不凋零，永遠不會向春光告別；
幸福的吹笛人，永不疲憊，
吹奏出的曲調總是那麼新鮮；
啊，更加幸福、更幸福的愛情！
永遠熱烈，永遠等待著縱情歡樂，
永遠悸動，永遠青春；
這所有活躍的人間情感：
徒留厭倦和悲傷於心，
頭腦發燙，唇乾舌燥。

Ah, happy, happy boughs! that cannot shed
Your leaves, nor ever bid the Spring adieu;
And, happy melodist, unwearied,
For ever piping songs for ever new;
More happy love! more happy, happy love!
For ever warm and still to be enjoy'd,
For ever panting, and for ever young;
All breathing human passion far above,
That leaves a heart high-sorrowful and cloy'd,
A burning forehead, and a parching tongue.

是誰前往獻祭？

佈滿綠意的祭壇，喔，神祕的祭司，

你牽領的牛犢正對天哀喚，

而她身旁又為何綴滿花環？

這些清晨祭神的虔誠信徒

是來自哪個傍水的小鎮，

還是幽靜堡寨中的山村？

啊，小鎮，你的街道永遠安靜，

也就無人得以講述，

你為何如此寂寥，從無人返。

Who are these coming to the sacrifice?
To what green altar, O mysterious priest,
Lead'st thou that heifer lowing at the skies,
And all her silken flanks with garlands drest?
What little town by river or sea shore,
Or mountain-built with peaceful citadel,
Is emptied of this folk, this pious morn?
And, little town, thy streets for evermore
Will silent be; and not a soul to tell
Why thou art desolate, can e'er return.

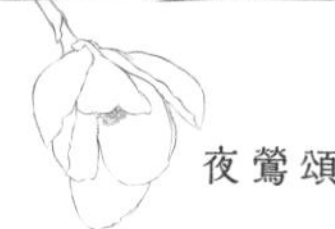

啊，雅典的形體！唯美的儀態！
刻有男人、女人的石雕，
還有林中樹枝及受人踐踏的草地；
你，安靜的形體，教我們超越思想，
有如永恆：清冷的牧歌！
當我們這一代衰老時，
只有你依然如故，在其他人的
悲傷中，你會安慰後人說：
「美即是真，真即是美」——這就是
你們所知道，和你們應該知道的一切。

O Attic shape! fair attitude! with brede
Of marble men and maidens overwrought,
With forest branches and the trodden weed;
Thou, silent form, dost tease us out of thought
As doth eternity: Cold Pastoral!
When old age shall this generation waste,
Thou shalt remain, in midst of other woe
Than ours, a friend to man, to whom thou say'st,
"Beauty is truth, truth beauty," – that is all
Ye know on earth, and all ye need to know.

幻想／

永遠讓幻想遨遊，

快樂總在外遊蕩：

稍一碰觸，快樂就會化為虛無，

如雨中的泡沫；

那麼就讓幻想乘著翅膀，

穿越那不斷擴展的思想：

打開心靈的大門，

她會衝上雲霧繚繞的天際；

哦，甜蜜的幻想啊！讓她解脫，

夏天的歡愉已享受殆盡，

春天的樂趣也如

花落一般逝去；

秋天結的果實雖如紅唇

在霧氣露水中透出嫣紅，

但嚐過就會生厭，這該如何？

Fancy

Ever let the Fancy roam,

Pleasure never is at home:

At a touch sweet Pleasure melteth,

Like to bubbles when rain pelteth;

Then let wingèd Fancy wander

Through the thought still spread beyond her:

Open wide the mind's cage-door,

She'll dart forth, and cloudward soar.

O sweet Fancy! let her loose;

Summer's joys are spoilt by use,

And the enjoying of the Spring

Fades as does its blossoming;

Autumn's red-lipp'd fruitage too,

Blushing through the mist and dew,

Cloys with tasting: What do then?

請你在火爐旁坐下，
看著熊熊燃燒的乾柴，
如同冬夜裡歡跳的精靈；
一片寂靜無聲的原野，
被平整厚實的雪覆蓋著，
耕童穿著厚重的鞋子。
此時，黑夜和白天
正在祕密謀劃
如何將黃昏逐出天際，
你只要坐著，
讓心靈沉靜，
派遣幻想，她使命必達——就派她去，
有奴僕為她執行任務；

Sit thee by the ingle, when
The sear faggot blazes bright,
Spirit of a winter's night;
When the soundless earth is muffled,
And the cakèd snow is shuffled.
From the ploughboy's heavy shoon;
When the Night doth meet the Noon
In a dark conspiracy
To banish Even from her sky.
Sit thee there, and send abroad,
With a mind self-overaw'd,
Fancy, high-commission'd: – send her!
She has vassals to atten'd her:

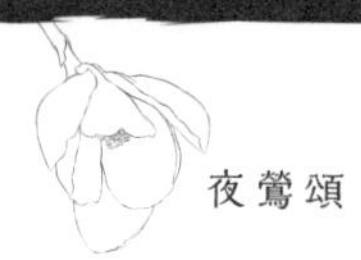

她不怕寒霜，因為她能喚回
大地已失去的嬌媚；
她還能喚回
夏日的歡欣喜悅。
在荊棘和草叢中採下
五月的蓓蕾和花冠；
秋天裡豐盈的收穫，
像是被祕密偷來的；
她會讓各種樂趣混為一體，
就像將三種瓊漿調成一杯，
乾杯吧——你將清楚聽到
遠處傳來的收穫歌聲，

She will bring, in spite of frost,
Beauties that the earth hath lost;
She will bring thee, all together,
All delights of summer weather;
All the buds and bells of May,
From dewy sward or thorny spray;
All the heapèd Autumn's wealth,
With a still, mysterious stealth:
She will mix these pleasures up
Like three fit wines in a cup,
And thou shalt quaff it: – thou shalt hear
Distant harvest-carols clear;

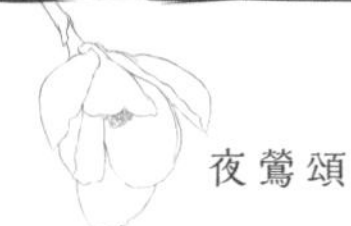

稻穀間發出窸窣聲響；

清晨鳥兒甜美的歌聲；

此刻，你聽——是雲雀！

正在初春的四月鳴叫，

還有正在尋覓樹枝和稻草的

烏鴉在聒噪。

只需一瞥，你就能夠看見

盛開的雛菊和金盞花；

白色的百合花，籬笆旁

初綻的櫻草；

隱匿的風信子，永遠是

五月中旬的藍寶石王后；

每片葉子、每朵花兒，

都有雨露為它們掛滿珍珠。

Rustle of the reapèd corn;
Sweet birds antheming the morn:
And, in the same moment-hark!
'Tis the early April lark,
Or the rooks, with busy caw,
Foraging for sticks and straw.
Thou shalt, at one glance, behold
The daisy and the marigold;
White-plumed lilies, and the first
Hedge-grown primrose that hath burst;
Shaded hyacinth, alway
Sapphire queen of the mid-May;
And every leaf, and every flower
Pearlèd with the self-same shower.

你還會看到甦醒的
田鼠，正在四處窺探；
冬眠過後的瘦蛇，
在陽光照耀的岸邊褪皮；
你會看到山楂樹間，雌鳥安歇
在滿佈青苔的巢中，
靜靜孵育著
斑駁紋路的卵；
隨後而來的蜜蜂，
引來了一陣騷動和恐懼；
在秋風輕柔的歌聲中，
成熟的橡果被打落在地上。

Thou shalt see the fieldmouse peep
Meagre from its cellèd sleep;
And the snake all winter-thin
Cast on sunny bank its skin;
Freckled nest-eggs thou shalt see
Hatching in the hawthorn-tree,
When the hen-bird's wing doth rest
Quiet on her mossy nest;
Then the hurry and alarm
When the beehive casts its swarm;
Acorns ripe down-pattering
While the autumn breezes sing.

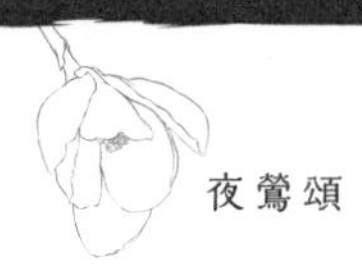

甜蜜的幻想啊，讓她解脫！

一切都會日益憔悴：

哪裡有青春的臉龐，

能永遠引人注目？哪一位少女的雙唇，

能永遠嬌艷欲滴？

哪一雙幽藍的眸子，

能永遠不疲憊？哪樣的容顏，

能在各處都能看見？

哪一種嬌柔的聲音，

能永遠聽起來婉約如昔？

稍一碰觸，快樂就會化為虛無，

如雨中的泡沫。

O sweet Fancy! let her loose;
Every thing is spoilt by use:
Where's the cheek that doth not fade,
Too much gazed at? Where's the maid
Whose lip mature is ever new?
Where's the eye, however blue,
Doth not weary? Where's the face
One would meet in every place?
Where's the voice, however soft,
One would hear so very oft?
At a touch sweet Pleasure melteth
Like to bubbles when rain pelteth.

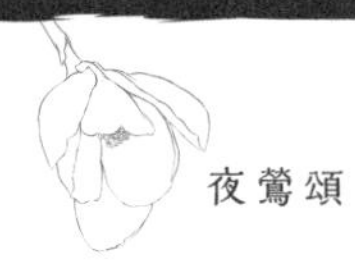

那麼，讓幻想乘著翅膀，

幫你尋個心儀的姑娘：

她擁有賽瑞斯的女兒那般柔媚的雙眸，

因為她不曾從痛苦之神那學來

如何皺眉，如何責罰；

她擁有如赫柏般

潔白的腰身，

當她腰帶上的金扣脫落，

上衣滑落於腳前，

手中還捧著醇香的佳釀，

朱比特迷醉了。——快解開

束縛著幻想的絲帶；

只要粉碎她的牢獄，

她就能帶來許多歡愉。——

永遠讓幻想遨遊，

快樂總在外遊蕩。

Let, then, wing Fancy find
Thee a mistress to thy mind:
Dulcet-eyed as Ceres' daughter,
Ere the God of Torment taught her
How to frown and how to chide;
With a waist and with a side
White as Hebe's, when her zone
Slipt its golden clasp, and down
Fell her kirtle to her feet,
While she held the goblet sweet,
And Jove grew languid. – Break the mesh
Of the Fancy's silken leash;
Quickly break her prison-string,
And such joys as these she'll bring. –
Let the wingèd Fancy roam,
Pleasure never is at home.

詩人頌／

歌詠激情和歡樂的詩人，
你們將靈魂留在了人間！
你們的靈魂是否也在天堂裡，
在新的世界過著雙重生活？
是的，你們在天的靈魂，
已成為日月的知己，
伴隨噴泉的神妙之聲，
與轟隆的雷聲一起震盪；
天堂的樹木颯颯作響，
彼此融洽地交談，
在極樂世界的草地上靜坐，
月神的小鹿在那吃草。

Ode

Bards of Passion and of Mirth,
Ye have left your souls on earth!
Have ye souls in heaven too,
Double lived in regions new?
Yes, and those of heaven commune
With the spheres of sun and moon;
With the noise of fountains wond'rous,
And the parle of voices thund'rous;
With the whisper of heaven's trees
And one another in soft ease
Seated on Elysian lawns
Brows'd by none but Dian's fawns;

藍色風鈴草如帷幕遮蔽；
雛菊散發出玫瑰般的芬芳，
但玫瑰有著獨特的馨香，
是世間不曾有過的馥鬱芳香；
夜鶯的啁啾婉轉，
不是無感的恍惚出神，
而是悅耳的無上真諦，
是智慧悠揚的樂曲，
是金色的歷史和傳說，
娓娓講述天堂的神祕與故事。
你們就這樣生活在天堂，
同時，你們也生活在世間；
你們留在世間的靈魂
教導人們如何找尋，
你們靈魂的另一所在，逍遙無邊，
永不倦怠，永不厭煩。

Underneath large blue-bells tented,
Where the daisies are rose-scented,
And the rose herself has got
Perfume which on earth is not;
Where the nightingale doth sing
Not a senseless, tranced thing,
But divine melodious truth;
Philosophic numbers smooth;
Tales and golden histories
Of heaven and its mysteries.
Thus ye live on high, and then
On the earth ye live again;
And the souls ye left behind you
Teach us, here the way to find you,
Where your other souls are joying,
Never slumber'd, never cloying.

這裡，你們留在世間的靈魂，

仍向人類講述著短暫的人生：

講述著悲傷與喜悅，

講述著愛恨與情仇，

講述著光榮與屈辱，

講述著力量與傷害。

你們就這樣，每天教導人們，

雖然遠離塵世，卻留下智慧。

歌詠激情和歡樂的詩人，

你們將靈魂留在了人間！

你們的靈魂是否也在天堂裡，

在新的世界過著雙重生活？

Here, your earth-born souls still speak
To mortals of their little week;
Of their sorrows and delights;
Of their passions and their spites;
Of their glory and their shame;
What doth strengthen and what maim.
Thus ye teach us, every day,
Wisdom though fled far away.
Bards of Passion and of Mirth,
Ye have left your souls on earth!
Ye have souls in heaven too,
Double lived in regions new!

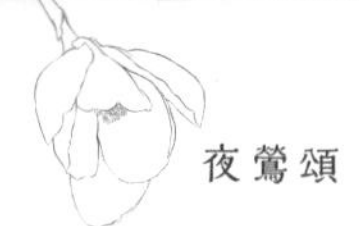

詠美人魚酒店／

啊，已故詩人的靈魂，
你們見過的極樂世界——
無論是快樂的田野或滿佈青苔的洞穴，
哪個能比得上美人魚酒店？
你們啜飲的佳釀，
哪比得上店主的葡萄酒？
就算是天堂裡的水果，
哪種能勝過
這鹿肉餅的美味？喔，豐盛的美食！
勇敢的羅賓漢將會
與他的瑪莉安
用角杯和瓶罐斟酒，啜飲品味。

Lines on the Mermaid Tavern

Souls of Poets dead and gone,
What Elysium have ye known –
Happy field or mossy cavern,
Choicer than the Mermaid Tavern?
Have ye tippled drink more fine
Than mine host's Canary wine?
Or are fruits of Paradise
Sweeter than those dainty pies
Of venison? O generous food!
Drest as though bold Robin Hood
Would, with his maid Marian,
Sup and bowse from horn and can.

我曾聽說，有一天，
店主的招牌不翼而飛，
沒人知道它去了哪裡，
直到占星師用他的鵝毛筆，
在羊皮紙上講出了故事。
他說，你們身著華服，
正在新的舊招牌底下，
啜飲著神仙的美酒，
歡欣慶祝美人魚酒店
開在了黃道帶上。

啊，已故詩人的靈魂，
你們見過的極樂世界——
無論是快樂的田野或滿佈青苔的洞穴，
哪個能比得上美人魚酒店？

I have heard that on a day
Mine host's sign-board flew away,
Nobody knew whither, till
An astrologer's old quill
To a sheepskin gave the story,
Said he saw you in your glory,
Underneath a new-old sign
Sipping beverage divine,
And pledging with contented smack
The Mermaid in the Zodiac.

Souls of Poets dead and gone,
What Elysium have ye known –
Happy field or mossy cavern
Choicer than the Mermaid Tavern?

秋頌／

霧靄朦朧和果實成熟的季節，
使萬物成熟的太陽是你的密友；
你們正偷偷謀劃著怎樣用纍纍
果實，掛滿茅屋下的藤蔓；
壓彎茅屋前的蘋果枝椏，
讓果實熟透至果核；
讓瓜果膨脹，讓榛果的外殼
包進甜蜜的果仁；讓遲開的花朵
綻放花苞，吸引蜜蜂，
讓它們以為溫暖的時光將長駐，
以為夏季已從飽滿的蜂巢裡溢出。

To Autumn

Season of mists and mellow fruitfulness,
Close bosom-friend of the maturi ng sun;
Conspiring with him how to load and bless
With fruit the vines that round the thatch-eaves run;
To bend with apples the moss'd cottage-trees,
And fill all fruit with ripeness to the core;
To swell the gourd, and plump the hazel shells
With a sweet kernel; to set budding more,
And still more, later flowers for the bees,
Until they think warm days will never cease,
For Summer has o'er-brimm'd their clammy cells.

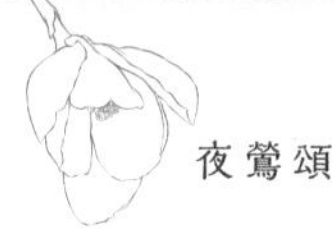

誰不曾在穀倉裡遇過你？
有時候在外面可以看到
你不經心地坐在穀倉的地上，
髮絲在揚穀的風中飄舞；
或在收割一半的稻田裡酣睡，
有時則會被罌粟的花香所醺醉，
讓鐮刀在罌粟花旁休憩；
或者，你背著穀袋，像拾穗人
跨過小溪，在水中投下倩影，
或者在榨蘋果汁的機器旁靜坐，
耐心地看那漸漸滴下的果漿。

Who hath not seen thee oft amid thy store?
Sometimes whoever seeks abroad may find
Thee sitting careless on a granary floor,
Thy hair sort-lifted by the winnowing wind;
Or on a half-reap'd furrow sound asleep,
Dows'd with the fume of poppies, while thy hook
Spares the next swath and all its twined flowers;
And sometimes like a gleaner thou dost keep
Steady thy laden head across a brook;
Or by a cyder-press, with patient look,
Thou watchest the last oozings hours by hours.

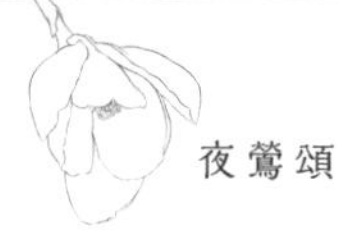

春天裡的歌聲去哪了？啊，他們在哪裡呢？
不要想這些，你也有自己的音樂：
當霞光映照即將逝去的天空，
給收割後殘留的田野抹上嫣紅，
接著，河邊柳樹旁的小蟲們
開始哀鳴，
忽上忽下，忽飛忽落；
蟋蟀在籬邊歌唱著，紅胸的
知更鳥在園中也高聲鳴囀著；
成群的羔羊在山中高聲咩叫，
群飛的燕子在空中吱吱喳喳。

Where are the songs of Spring? Ay, where are they?
Think not of them, thou hast thy music too, –
While barr clouds bloom the soft-dying day,
And touch the stubble-plains with rosy hue;
Then in a wailful choir the small gnats mourn
Among the river sallows, borne aloft
Or sinking as the light wind lives or dies;
And full-grown lambs loud bleat from hilly bourn;
Hedge-crickets sing; and now with treble soft
The red-breast whistles form a garden-croft;
And gathering swallows twitter in the skies.

憂鬱頌／

不，不要到忘川去，

不要把附子草的毒汁當成美酒；

不要讓龍葵，那普羅塞庇娜的紅葡萄，

親吻你的額頭，

不要把紫杉果做成念珠，

不要把甲蟲或者飛蛾

當作哀憐你的賽姬，也不要

把你心底的祕密洩漏給毛茸茸的貓頭鷹；

因為陰影與陰影親近，更會

心生困倦，讓靈魂不再清醒。

Ode on Melancholy

No, no, go not to Lethe, neither twist
Wolf's-bane, tight-rooted, for its poisonous wine;
Nor suffer thy pale forehead to be kiss'd
By nightshade, ruby grape of Proserpine;
Make not your rosary of yew-berries,
Nor let the beetle, nor the death-moth be
Your mournful Psyche, nor the downy owl
A partner in your sorrow's mysteries;
For shade to shade will come too drowsily,
And drown the wakeful anguish of the soul.

一旦憂鬱的情緒來襲，

就像天上哭泣的烏雲，

用淚水滋潤著萎靡的花草，

以四月的白霧繚繞翠峰；

你早就該讓清晨的玫瑰

或花團錦簇的牡丹，來滋潤你的哀愁，

或者，給哀愁披去海浪上的彩虹。

要是你的姑娘嗔怒了，

就拉住她的玉手，讓她宣洩，

並且深深、深深地注視她美麗的眼。

But when the melancholy fit shall fall
Sudden from heaven like a weeping cloud,
That fosters the droop-headed flowers all,
And hides the green hill in an April shroud;
Then glut thy sorrow on a morning rose,
Or on the rainbow of the salt sand-wave,
Or on the wealth of globed peonies;
Or if thy mistress some rich anger shows,
Emprison her soft hand, and let her rave,
And feed deep, deep upon her peerless eyes.

她與美共生死——那終會消亡的美，
還有喜悅，道別時，他的手指總是
觸碰著美麗的唇；
令人痛苦的喜悅隨侍在旁，
只要蜜蜂啜一口，就會變為毒汁：
在快樂殿堂中隱蔽的憂鬱，
有她自己的神龕，
雖然，只有舌頭靈敏、味覺健全，
能咬破喜悅之果的人才能看見；
他的靈魂一旦碰到憂鬱，
就會立即被俘獲，並高掛於雲端。

She dwells with Beauty – Beauty that must die;
And Joy, whose hand is ever at his lips
Bidding adieu; and aching Pleasure nigh,
Turning to Poison while the bee-mouth sips:
Ay, in the very temple of delight
Veil'd Melancholy has her sovran shrine,
Though seen of none save him whose strenuous tongue
Can burst Joy's grape against his palate fine;
His soul shall taste the sadness of her might,
And be among her cloudy trophies hung.

阿波羅禮贊／

神啊，你擁有金弓，
擁有金色的琴，
擁有金色的頭髮，
還有金色的火焰，
駕著車在四季的旅途中
慢慢前行；
哪裡——你將怒火埋藏在哪裡？
難道你能忍受像我這樣的傻瓜戴上
你的花環，你的桂冠，你的榮耀，
你故事的光彩？
或者，我是蠕蟲——將緩慢爬向死亡？
哦，德爾菲的阿波羅！

God of the Golden Bow

God of the golden bow,

And of the golden lyre,

And of the golden hair,

And of the golden fire,

Charioteer

Of the patient year,

Where – where slept thine ire,

When like a blank idiot I put on thy wreath,

Thy laurel, thy glory,

The light of thy story,

Or was I a worm – too low crawling for death?

O Delphic Apollo!

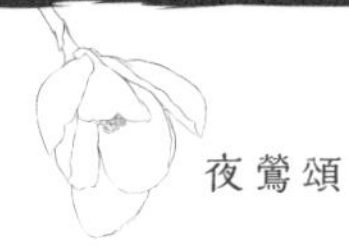

雷神握拳再握拳，
雷神皺眉又皺眉；
雄鷹的羽毛像鬃毛般
怒髮衝冠。而雷電
才開始醞釀它的聲響，
就漸漸消沉下去，
無拘無束地喋喋不休。
喔，為什麼你要同情，還為蠕蟲求情？
為什麼要輕彈你的金琴，
讓雷聲靜默，
為什麼不讓它摧毀我——這可悲的萌芽？
哦，德爾菲的阿波羅！

The Thunderer grasp'd and grasp'd,

The Thunderer frown'd and frown'd;

The eagle's feathery mane

For wrath became stiffen'd – the sound

Of breeding thunder

Went drowsily under,

Muttering to be unbound.

O why didst thou pity, and beg for a worm?

Why touch thy soft lute

Till the thunder was mute,

Why was I not crush'd – such a pitiful germ?

O Delphic Apollo!

注視著寧靜的氣流，

大地上的種子和樹根，

為了夏日的盛宴而日漸茁壯；

大地的近鄰，海洋

重複著亙古不變的勞作，

此時，誰——有誰膽敢

打成平手，在他的額前種植

驕傲地嘲笑，

高聲地辱罵，

引以為榮，向你卑躬屈膝，

哦，德爾菲的阿波羅！

Watching the silent air;
The seeds and roots in Earth
Were swelling for summer fare;
The Ocean, its neighbour,
Was at his old labour,
When, who – who did dare
To tie for a moment, thy plant round his brow,
And grin and look proudly,
And blaspheme so loudly,
And live for that honour, to stoop to thee now?
O Delphic Apollo!

無情的妖女／

騎士啊，什麼讓你如此苦惱，
面色蒼白，獨自沮喪彷徨？
湖邊的蘆葦已經枯萎，
鳥兒也不再歌唱。

騎士啊，什麼讓你如此苦惱，
你面容憔悴，充滿憂傷？
松鼠的小窩儲滿了食物，
糧食也裝進了穀倉。

你的額頭白得像百合花，
滲出的汗水如顆顆露珠，
你的臉頰就像
正在凋謝的玫瑰花。

La Belle Sans Meraci: a Ballad

O what can ail thee, kings at arms,
Alone and palely loitering?
The sedge has wither'd from the lake,
And no birds sing.

O what can ail thee, kings at arms,
So haggard and so woe-begone?
The squirrel's granary is full,
And the Harvest's done.

I see a lily on thy brow
With anguish moist and fever dew,
And no thy cheeks a fading rose
Fast withered too.

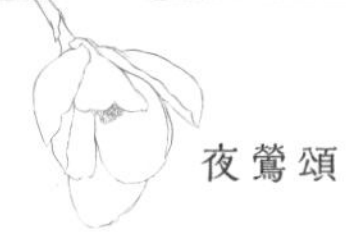

在草坪中，我看見了一名女子，
她美得像天仙的子女，
有著飄逸的長髮、輕盈的步伐，
眼睛裡卻閃耀著狂放的光芒。

我為她編織了一頂花帽、
手鐲和芬芳的腰帶，
她彷彿真的愛我，凝視
並輕柔地發出嘆息。

我帶她漫步街道，
一整天除了她我什麼都看不見，
沿路只有她擺身，歌唱
那天仙的歌曲。

I met a lady in the meads,
Full beautiful, and a fairy's child;
Her hair was long, her foot was light,
And her eyes were wild.

I made a garland for her head,
And bracelets too, and Fragrant zone;
She looked at me as she did love,
And made sweet moan.

I set her on my pacing street,
And nothing else saw all day long,
For sidelong would she bend, and sing
A fairy's song.

她為我採拾美味的草根，
野地的蜂蜜和鮮果，
她用奇妙的語言對著我說——
說她真心愛我。

她帶我回去精靈般的洞穴，
在那裡她哭了起來，哀嘆連連
我四度親吻
才讓她閉上那狂放的眼。

She found me roots of relish sweet,
And honey wild, and manna dew,
And sure in languages strange she said –
I love thee true.

She took me to her elfin grot,
And there she wept, and sigh'd full score,
And there I shut here wild wild eyes
With kisses four.

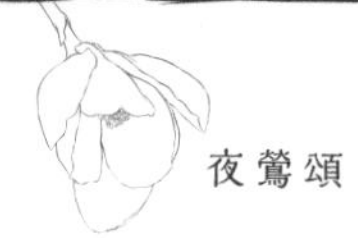

她讓我在洞穴中迷糊睡去，

我做了個夢——啊，不幸的預兆！

我未曾有過如此夢境，

身處冰冷的山邊。

我見到面色蒼白的國王及王子，

還有很多戰士，全都如死去般慘白；

他們哭號：「無情的妖女

已經將你囚禁！」

And there she lulled me asleep,
And there I dream'd – Ah! Woe betide!
The latest dream I ever dream'd
On the cold hill's side

I saw pale kings, and princes too,
Pale warriors, death pale were they all;
They cried – 'La belle dame sans merci
Hath thee in thrall!'

幽暗中我見到他們因飢餓而齜牙咧嘴，
發出可怕聲響，
我突然驚醒，發現自己，
身處冰冷的山邊。

這就是為何我在此逗留，
面色蒼白，獨自沮喪彷徨。
湖邊的蘆葦已經枯萎，
鳥兒也不再歌唱。

I saw their starved lips in the gloam,
With horrid warning gaped wide,
And I awoke and found me here,
On the cold hill's side.

And this is why I sojourn here
Alone and palely loitering,
Though the sedge is withered from the lake,
And no birds sing.

伊薩貝拉（〈羅勒花盆〉）——取自薄伽丘的故事／

I.

美麗的伊薩貝拉！純情的伊薩貝拉！
羅倫佐，崇尚愛情的年輕人！
他們同住在一幢豪華的大廈裡，
怎麼能不感到內心的悸動，相思成病？
他們坐下來共同進餐，相依相偎
怎會不稱心如意？
的確，他們雖在同一屋頂下入睡，
也必然會夢到彼此，夜夜飲泣。

II.

每到早晨，他們的愛情就更加溫柔，
每到傍晚，他們的感情溫柔依舊，更顯深切；
無論他走在室內、田野或花園，
她的倩影都會充滿他的眼簾；
她也如此，颯颯落葉，潺潺溪流的喧響
都比不上他情意綿綿的嗓音；
他的名字常常在她的琵琶上迴盪，
他的名字也讓她亂了手中的編織。

Isabella (The Pot of Basil)– A Story from Boccaccio

I.

Fair Isabel, poor simple Isabel!

Lorenzo, a young palmer in Love's eye!

They could not in the self-same mansion dwell

Without some stir of heart, some malady;

They could not sit at meals but feel how well

It soothed each to be the other by;

They could not, sure, beneath the same roof sleep

But to each other dream, and nightly weep.

II.

With every morn their love grew tenderer,

With every eve deeper and tenderer still;

He might not in house, field, or garden stir,

But her full shape would all his seeing fill;

And his continual voice was pleasanter

To her, than noise of trees or hidden rill;

Her lute-string gave an echo of his name,

She spoilt her half-done broidery with the same.

III.

她的身影還沒出現在他視線內，
他早已知道誰的玉手正握著門把；
他能看進她的閨房，欣賞她的美，
看得比鷹隼來得準確；
她做晚禱時，他總是守望著她，
她的面龐和他仰望著相同的天空：
他在相思中，熬過漫漫長夜，
只為傾聽她清早下樓的腳步聲。

IV.

漫長的五月都在相思中度過，
六月來了，他們的臉都變得更加蒼白，
「明天，要向我的可人兒鞠躬，」
「明天，要向我愛的姑娘請求青睞。」
「噢，羅倫佐，我願意今夜就死去，
如果你的雙唇還唱不出愛情的曲調。」
但是，唉，這只是他對著枕頭的低語。
他苦澀的日子，日復一日。

III.

He knew whose gentle hand was at the latch
Before the door had given her to his eyes;
And from her chamber-window he would catch
Her beauty farther than the falcon spies;
And constant as her vespers would he watch,
Because her face was turn'd to the same skies;
And with sick longing all the night outwear,
To hear her morning-step upon the stair.

IV.

A whole long month of May in this sad plight
Made their cheeks paler by the break of June:
"To-morrow will I bow to my delight,
"To-morrow will I ask my lady's boon." –
"O may I never see another night,
"Lorenzo, if thy lips breathe not love's tune." –
So spake they to their pillows; but, alas,
Honeyless days and days did he let pass;

V.

甜美的伊薩貝拉的雙頰
卻病奄奄地佈滿玫瑰般的紅暈，
如年輕母親般的清瘦，她輕輕唱著
催眠曲，以緩解嬰兒的病痛。
「啊，她病得這麼厲害！」他說，「我不該說，
可是我想宣告自己對她的愛情：
如果容顏透露了她的心事，我要將她的淚水吻去，
至少這樣能夠趕走她的煩憂。」

VI.

在一個美妙的清晨，他下定了決心，
一整天他都因激動而心跳加速；
他暗中為自己禱告，希望自己有膽量表白；
但奔湧的熱血，窒息了他的聲音，他決定再次推延——
雖然心中滿是對伊薩貝拉的思念，
在她面前，卻像個孩子般羞怯：
唉呀，愛情竟是這般膽怯和狂野！

V.

Until sweet Isabella's untouch'd cheek
Fell sick within the rose's just domain,
Fell thin as a young mother's, who doth seek
By every lull to cool her infant's pain:
"How ill she is," said he,"I may not speak,
"And yet I will, and tell my love all plain:
"If looks speak love—laws, I will drink her tears,
"And at the least 'twill startle off her cares."

VI.

So said he one fair morning, and all day
His heart beat awfully against his side;
And to his heart he inwardly did pray
For power to speak; but still the ruddy tide
Stifled his voice, and puls'd resolve away –
Fever'd his high conceit of such a bride,
Yet brought him to the meekness of a child:
Alas! when passion is both meek and wild!

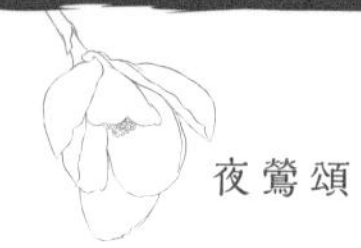

VII.

於是，他又一次在失眠中捱過
充滿相思與折磨的淒涼漫漫長夜，
如果說，伊薩貝拉的敏銳目光
看不出他眉宇間的變化，
她就不會見他蒼白呆滯死寂的神情，
就立刻羞紅了臉；滿是柔情地
小聲叫道：「羅倫佐！」──她欲言又止，
但是從她的語氣和神情，他就明白了一切。

VIII.

「啊，伊薩貝拉！我不能完全肯定
能否向你訴說悲哀；
假如你曾信過什麼，那請你相信：
我是多麼愛你，我的靈魂已瀕臨
毀滅。我不想魯莽地握緊，那會
壓疼你的手，也不願用大膽的注視來
冒犯你的眼睛；可是啊，如果我不向你傾訴我的情愫，
我將活不到明天！」

VII.

So once more he had wak'd and anguished
A dreary night of love and misery,
If Isabel's quick eye had not been wed
To every symbol on his forehead high;
She saw it waxing very pale and dead,
And straight all flush'd; so, lisped tenderly,
"Lorenzo!" – here she ceas'd her timid quest,
But in her tone and look he read the rest.

VIII.

"O Isabella, I can half perceive
"That I may speak my grief into thine ear;
"If thou didst ever anything believe,
"Believe how I love thee, believe how near
"My soul is to its doom: I would not grieve
"Thy hand by unwelcome pressing, would not fear
"Thine eyes by gazing; but I cannot live
"Another night, and not my passion shrive.

IX.

「愛情啊！你帶我走出了嚴寒，
女孩！你領我走進了盛夏，
我一定要品嚐沐浴著溫暖、
迎著朝陽盛開的鮮花。」
當此之際，他原本怯懦的嘴唇變得勇敢，
與她的嘴唇如韻腳般成詩：
他們無比地幸福和快樂
猶如在六月陽光照耀下活潑的花朵。

X.

分別時，他們幸福得飄飄然，
像是被和風吹開的兩朵並蒂玫瑰，
分離是為了更親密的相聚，
使彼此的馨香融合在一起。
她回到閨房，唱著優美的旋律，
歌唱著甜蜜的愛情和被愛的美妙；
而他則以輕快的步伐登上西山，
向太陽揮手告別，心中滿是歡喜。

IX.

"Love! thou art leading me from wintry cold,
"Lady! thou leadest me to summer clime,
"And I must taste the blossoms that unfold
"In its ripe warmth this gracious morning time."
So said, his erewhile timid lips grew bold,
And poesied with hers in dewy rhyme:
Great bliss was with them, and great happiness
Grew, like a lusty flower in June's caress.

X.

Parting they seem'd to tread upon the air,
Twin roses by the zephyr blown apart
Only to meet again more close, and share
The inward fragrance of each other's heart.
She, to her chamber gone, a ditty fair
Sang, of delicious love and honey'd dart;
He with light steps went up a western hill,
And bade the sun farewell, and joy'd his fill.

XI.

他們又再次祕密地會面，在黃昏
拉開華麗的帷幕，群星閃耀之前，
他們祕密地會面，在黃昏
拉開華麗的帷幕，群星閃耀之前，
在風信子和麝香的林蔭中祕密會面，
沒有人知曉，遠離流言蜚語。
啊！但願能夠永遠如此，免得無聊的人
反而因他們的悲傷而顯得快樂。

XII.

他們那時不快樂嗎？——絕不可能——
我們為戀人們流過了太多眼淚，
我們用太多的嘆息酬謝他們，
我們在他們死後給予太多惋惜，
我們看過太多悲傷的故事，
那些內容讀時閃耀著燦爛金光；
除了這頁內容寫到，特修斯的妻子
對著波浪遠望他的弓箭。

XI.

All close they met again, before the dusk
Had taken from the stars its pleasant veil,
All close they met, all eves, before the dusk
Had taken from the stars its pleasant veil,
Close in a bower of hyacinth and musk,
Unknown of any, free from whispering tale.
Ah! better had it been for ever so,
Than idle ears should pleasure in their woe.

XII.

Were they unhappy then? – It cannot be –
Too many tears for lovers have been shed,
Too many sighs give we to them in fee,
Too much of pity after they are dead,
Too many doleful stories do we see,
Whose matter in bright gold were best be read;
Except in such a page where Theseus' spouse
Over the pathless waves towards him bows.

XIII.

然而，愛情給予豐厚的獎賞，
片刻的甜蜜就可以抵銷長久的苦澀，
儘管蒂朵安息在墓中，
伊薩貝拉承受巨大的磨難，
儘管羅倫佐沒有被印度丁香樹
溫暖的氣息環繞，但是真理不變——
連蜜蜂，這些仰賴春天花苞的小小貧民，
都知道最甜美的汁液藏在有毒的花朵裡。

XIV.

這位美女跟兩個哥哥住在一起，
繼承了祖先的財富。
在火炬照耀的礦坑、喧鬧的工廠裡，
多少疲倦的雙手為他們揮汗如雨，
多少人曾經腰繫箭筒，
被鞭子抽打融化成血水——目光茫然
終日站在波光粼粼的河水裡，
只為了取得隨水流而來的金屬礦砂。

XIII.

But, for the general award of love,
The little sweet doth kill much bitterness;
Though Dido silent is in under-grove,
And Isabella's was a great distress,
Though young Lorenzo in warm Indian clove
Was not embalm'd, this truth is not the less –
Even bees, the little almsmen of spring-bowers,
Know there is richest juice in poison-flowers.

XIV.

With her two brothers this fair lady dwelt,
Enriched from ancestral merchandize,
And for them many a weary hand did swelt
In torched mines and noisy factories,
And many once proud-quiver'd loins did melt
In blood from stinging whip;—with hollow eyes
Many all day in dazzling river stood,
To take the rich-ored driftings of the flood.

XV.

錫蘭的潛水者為他們屏住呼吸
赤裸著身體挨近饑餓的鯊魚；
他的耳朵為他們淌著血；海豹為他們
在海岸上痛苦的呻吟著，渾身
插滿了箭，死於冰層上；無數的人為他們
在痛苦無邊的生活裡煎熬，
而他們過著悠閒的生活，全然不知：
自己正設下了工作的刑具折磨世人。

XVI.

他們憑什麼這樣驕傲？憑大理石噴泉的泉水
比可憐人的眼淚流得更驕傲嗎？
他們憑什麼這樣驕傲？憑整座山種滿柑橘？
難道它比乞丐爬著的臺階更容易攀登嗎？
他們憑什麼這樣驕傲？憑著有註銷的帳單？
難道它比古希臘的詩歌更富有嗎？
他們憑什麼這樣驕傲？我們高聲問，
為什麼他們能以榮譽之名那麼驕傲？

XV.

For them the Ceylon diver held his breath,
And went all naked to the hungry shark;
For them his ears gush'd blood; for them in death
The seal on the cold ice with piteous bark
Lay full of darts; for them alone did seethe
A thousand men in troubles wide and dark:
Half-ignorant, they turn'd an easy wheel,
That set sharp racks at work, to pinch and peel.

XVI.

Why were they proud? Because their marble founts
Gush'd with more pride than do a wretch's tears? –
Why were they proud? Because fair orange-mounts
Were of more soft ascent than lazar stairs? –
Why were they proud? Because red-lin'd accounts
Were richer than the songs of Grecian years? –
Why were they proud? again we ask aloud,
Why in the name of Glory were they proud?

XVII.

然而這兩個佛羅倫斯商人卻憑藉
貪婪般的傲慢和掠奪式的懦弱逍遙於外，
像是來自聖地的兩個吝嗇希伯來人，
圍起葡萄園防止乞丐來探看，
他們像盤旋在船桅的鷹隼，
像馱不盡金銀財寶與謊言的騾與馬，
像貓爪迅速撲向離群的肥鼠，
掌控西班牙、托斯卡尼和馬來人。

XVIII.

這樣兩個商人怎麼猜得出
伊薩貝拉溫柔的祕密？
他們怎會發現羅倫佐的眼睛
有著心不在焉的神態？讓埃及的瘟疫
闖入他們貪婪而狡猾的視線吧！
兩個守財奴怎麼能分清是與非？
他們竟然做到了——如同被追趕的野兔，
真正的商人都必前瞻後顧。

XVII.

Yet were these Florentines as self-retired
In hungry pride and gainful cowardice,
As two close Hebrews in that land inspired,
Paled in and vineyarded from beggar-spies;
The hawks of ship – mast forests – the untired
And pannier'd mules for ducats and old lies –
Quick cat's-paws on the generous stray-away, –
Great wits in Spanish, Tuscan, and Malay.

XVIII.

How was it these same ledger-men could spy
Fair Isabella in her downy nest?
How could they find out in Lorenzo's eye
A straying from his toil? Hot Egypt's pest
Into their vision covetous and sly!
How could these money-bags see east and west? –
Yet so they did – and every dealer fair
Must see behind, as doth the hunted hare.

XIX.

啊，擅辯且有名的薄伽丘！

現在我們懇求你的寬宏大量，

請求你那盛開的香花原諒，

請求你那迷戀月亮的玫瑰花原諒，

請求你那因聽不到琴聲而蒼白的

百合也寬恕一次。

這魯莽的辭句，實在難於

表現這段陰鬱的悲劇主題。

XX.

只要得到你的諒解，這故事一定會

順利地講述下去，有條不紊；

我雖然拙劣，卻沒有妄想

把古代的文章化為更美的詩律：

但我還是寫了——無論好壞——

只對你的在天之靈表示敬仰；

只為在英文詩中表現你的風格，

讓北國的風中迴響起你的歌聲。

XIX.

O eloquent and famed Boccaccio!

Of thee we now should ask forgiving boon,

And of thy spicy myrtles as they blow,

And of thy roses amorous of the moon,

And of thy lillies, that do paler grow

Now they can no more hear thy ghittern's tune,

For venturing syllables that ill beseem

The quiet glooms of such a piteous theme.

XX.

Grant thou a pardon here, and then the tale

Shall move on soberly, as it is meet;

There is no other crime, no mad assail

To make old prose in modern rhyme more sweet:

But it is done – succeed the verse or fail –

To honour thee, and thy gone spirit greet;

To stead thee as a verse in English tongue,

An echo of thee in the north—wind sung.

XXI.

兩兄弟從諸多端倪中有所察覺，
羅倫佐深深地愛上了自己妹妹，
而妹妹也愛著他，這使他們
彼此發洩不滿，後來竟感到憤怒：
因為他只是他們生意中的一名奴僕，
竟然能享受妹妹的忠貞愛情！
而他們正謀劃勸誘妹妹接受
一位富有的貴族，和他的橄欖樹莊園。

XXII.

無數次，他們在嫉妒地商量，
無數次，他們咬著自己的嘴唇，
終於想出了萬無一失的辦法，
要叫那年輕人以命抵過；
這兩個兇殘的人啊，簡直是
用尖刀刺碎了善良的靈魂，
他們決定，要在幽暗的樹林裡
殺死羅倫佐，並把他掩埋滅跡。

XXI.

These brethren having found by many signs
What love Lorenzo for their sister had,
And how she lov'd him too, each unconfines
His bitter thoughts to other, well nigh mad
That he, the servant of their trade designs,
Should in their sister's love be blithe and glad,
When 'twas their plan to coax her by degrees
To some high noble and his olive-trees.

XXII.

And many a jealous conference had they,
And many times they bit their lips alone,
Before they fix'd upon a surest way
To make the youngster for his crime atone;
And at the last, these men of cruel clay
Cut Mercy with a sharp knife to the bone;
For they resolved in some forest dim
To kill Lorenzo, and there bury him.

XXIII.

在一個晴朗的早晨，正當他
在園中倚著花園上的欄杆
遠眺日出之時，他們足跡踏過了露珠，
走到他面前說：
「羅倫佐，你好像是在享受
生活的恬靜，我們不願擾亂
你寧靜的遐想，可是，假如你聰明的話，
騎上駿馬去馳騁吧，趁天氣還這麼涼爽。」

XXIV.

「我們想在今天，不，就現在
三人一起騎馬，往亞平寧山脈過去；
來吧，我們求你，趁著炎熱的太陽
還沒有把薔薇上的露珠數完。」
羅倫佐，他如往常般儒雅，
躬一躬身，答應了這對蛇蠍，
便趕忙去準備行裝了：
繫緊腰帶、靴刺、穿上獵人的服裝。

XXIII.

So on a pleasant morning, as he leant
Into the sun-rise, o'er the balustrade
Of the garden-terrace, towards him they bent
Their footing through the dews; and to him said,
"You seem there in the quiet of content,
"Lorenzo, and we are most loth to invade
"Calm speculation; but if you are wise,
"Bestride your steed while cold is in the skies.

XXIV.

"To-day we purpose, aye, this hour we mount
"To spur three leagues towards the Apennine;
"Come down, we pray thee, ere the hot sun count
"His dewy rosary on the eglantine."
Lorenzo, courteously as he was wont,
Bow'd a fair greeting to these serpents' whine;
And went in haste, to get in readiness,
With belt, and spur, and bracing huntsman's dress.

XXV.

而當他向庭院走去的時候，
每走三步就停下來，細心傾聽
是否有心愛女孩的晨歌，
或聽見她輕柔腳步的絲絲細語；
正當他在熱烈的愛情中流連，
他聽到來自上面悅耳的笑聲：
他抬起頭看見了光彩照人的姑娘，
正在窗櫺裡微笑，秀麗猶如天仙。

XXVI.

「伊薩貝拉，我的愛！」他說，「我真痛苦，」
「唯恐來不及對你道一聲早安。
唉！只分別了三小時我就忍受不住
各種憂慮的煎熬，假如我真的
失去了你，我可怎麼辦？但我們仍能
從愛情的幽暗走進愛情的白天。
再見了！我很快就回來。」──「再見！」她說。
他離開的時候，她快樂地歌唱。

XXV.

And as he to the court-yard pass'd along,
Each third step did he pause, and listen'd oft
If he could hear his lady's matin-song,
Or the light whisper of her footstep soft;
And as he thus over his passion hung,
He heard a laugh full musical aloft;
When, looking up, he saw her features bright
Smile through an in-door lattice, all delight.

XXVI.

"Love, Isabel!" said he, "I was in pain
"Lest I should miss to bid thee a good morrow:
"Ah! what if I should lose thee, when so fain
"I am to stifle all the heavy sorrow
"Of a poor three hours' absence? but we'll gain
"Out of the amorous dark what day doth borrow.
"Good bye! I'll soon be back." – "Good bye!" said she.
And as he went she chanted merrily.

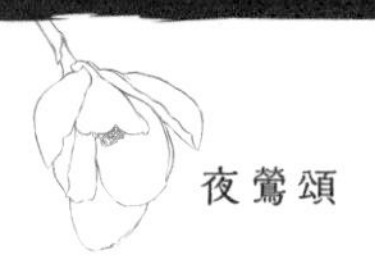

XXVII.

於是，兄弟倆和他們要謀殺的人
騎馬走出了佛羅倫斯，到了亞諾河邊；
河水在狹窄的山谷中奔流，
岸邊的蘆葦歡躍地搖擺著，
而鯽魚正在逆水前行。兩兄弟
涉水過河時，臉上都蒼白失色，
羅倫佐的臉上則充滿了愛情的紅潤。——他們過了河，
來到幽靜的樹林之中，準備一場屠殺。

XXVIII.

羅倫佐就此被殺害和掩埋，
就在樹林裡，結束了他高尚的愛情；
啊！靈魂脫離軀體，得到解放，
卻在孤寂中悲痛：不得安寧，
正如犯罪的惡狗。
兩兄弟在河裡洗淨自己的劍，
然後猛烈地策馬回家，
他們殺了人，卻變得更加富裕。

XXVII.

So the two brothers and their murder'd man
Rode past fair Florence, to where Arno's stream
Gurgles through straiten'd banks, and still doth fan
Itself with dancing bulrush, and the bream
Keeps head against the freshets. Sick and wan
The brothers' faces in the ford did seem,
Lorenzo's flush with love. – They pass'd the water
Into a forest quiet for the slaughter.

XXVIII.

There was Lorenzo slain and buried in,
There in that forest did his great love cease;
Ah! when a soul doth thus its freedom win,
It aches in loneliness – is ill at peace
As the break-covert blood-hounds of such sin:
They dipp'd their swords in the water, and did tease
Their horses homeward, with convulsed spur,
Each richer by his being a murderer.

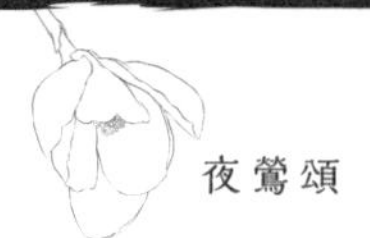

XXIX.

他們告訴妹妹，羅倫佐是如何
急急忙忙地乘船到國外，處理
緊急的商務，他們只有
這位可信賴的人能賦予重任，
可憐的女孩！披上你寡婦的哀服吧，
掙開希望給予詛咒的枷鎖；
今天你不能看見他，明天也不能，
下一個日子你仍是滿心悲痛。

XXX.

她獨自一人，為失去的歡樂而
哭泣，哭到夜幕降臨；
而那時，愛情已消失，喔，徒留悲傷！
她只好獨自回想著往日情懷：
在幽暗中，她彷彿看見他的影子，
在寂靜中她輕輕地發出悲鳴；
接著把完美的雙臂舉向空中，
在臥榻上喃喃說著：「哪裡？喔，在哪裡？」

XXIX.

They told their sister how, with sudden speed,
Lorenzo had ta'en ship for foreign lands,
Because of some great urgency and need
In their affairs, requiring trusty hands.
Poor Girl! put on thy stifling widow's weed,
And 'scape at once from Hope's accursed bands;
To-day thou wilt not see him, nor to-morrow,
And the next day will be a day of sorrow.

XXX.

She weeps alone for pleasures not to be;
Sorely she wept until the night came on,
And then, instead of love, O misery!
She brooded o'er the luxury alone:
His image in the dusk she seem'd to see,
And to the silence made a gentle moan,
Spreading her perfect arms upon the air,
And on her couch low murmuring "Where? O where?"

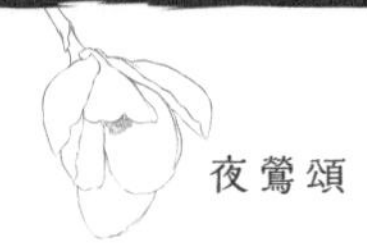

XXXI.

但自私——愛情的表親，——沒多久就
在她專一的胸中點燃愛情的火焰；
她曾因為期待黃金時刻而焦躁不安，
焦急地挨過那孤寂的時光，
但沒多久，她內心
被強烈的感情所佔據，
悲劇降臨：那抑制不住的真情，
為戀人貿然遠行而悲痛。

XXXII.

到了仲秋時節，每逢黃昏，
從遠方飄來了寒冷的氣息，
病懨懨的西方天空失去了
金黃色彩，還在灌木叢間
奏出死亡之歌，催促簌簌的葉子
趕快凋零；然後冬天才敢
走出北方的岩洞。
伊薩貝拉的美麗正逐漸枯萎失色。

XXXI.

But Selfishness, Love's cousin, held not long
Its fiery vigil in her single breast;
She fretted for the golden hour, and hung
Upon the time with feverish unrest –
Not long – for soon into her heart a throng
Of higher occupants, a richer zest,
Came tragic; passion not to be subdued,
And sorrow for her love in travels rude.

XXXII.

In the mid days of autumn, on their eves
The breath of Winter comes from far away,
And the sick west continually bereaves
Of some gold tinge, and plays a roundelay
Of death among the bushes and the leaves,
To make all bare before he dares to stray
From his north cavern. So sweet Isabel
By gradual decay from beauty fell,

XXXIII.

因為羅倫佐沒有回來，

她的眼睛已失去了光澤。

好幾次她問哥哥們，究竟他去了哪個地牢，

才遲遲未歸？為了使她心安，

他們用一個個謊言安慰她。他們的罪惡

像欣諾姆谷地的煙在心中迴旋；

每天夜裡，他們都在夢裡悲鳴，

似乎看見妹妹身披著雪白的壽衣。

XXXIV.

或許她到死都茫然無知，

要不是有一個最難測的暗示：

它恰如偶然飲下的強烈藥物，

使病危的人可以多停留片刻，

不致立刻死去；它宛如長矛

以殘酷的一刺，使印度人從雲霧的

樓閣中醒來，使他再次感受

烈火在心中和腦中嚙咬。

XXXIII.

Because Lorenzo came not. Oftentimes
She ask'd her brothers, with an eye all pale,
Striving to be itself, what dungeon climes
Could keep him off so long? They spake a tale
Time after time, to quiet her. Their crimes
Came on them, like a smoke from Hinnom's vale;
And every night in dreams they groan'd aloud,
To see their sister in her snowy shroud.

XXXIV.

And she had died in drowsy ignorance,
But for a thing more deadly dark than all;
It came like a fierce potion, drunk by chance,
Which saves a sick man from the feather'd pall
For some few gasping moments; like a lance,
Waking an Indian from his cloudy hall
With cruel pierce, and bringing him again
Sense of the gnawing fire at heart and brain.

XXXV.

這是夢境。在最深沉的午夜，
在幽暗的午夜裡，羅倫佐站在
她的床邊，流著淚：林中的墳墓
玷污了他髮稍曾閃耀的光彩；
凜冽的寒冷封住了他的唇；
他淒涼的嗓音，失去了過往悠揚的聲調；
被泥土覆蓋的耳際
劃出一條小溝，眼淚流淌而下。

XXXVI.

幽靈竟然開口了，發出了怪異的聲音：
因為它那笨拙的舌頭想發出
從前那悅耳的嗓音，
伊薩貝拉仔細聽著那聲調：
就像一雙麻木的雙手彈著破琴，
音律不協調，又像因無力而變得飄渺；
幽靈的歌聲在他口中嗚咽著，
猶如瑟瑟夜風從陰森多刺的墳場穿過。

XXXV.

It was a vision. – In the drowsy gloom,
The dull of midnight, at her couch's foot
Lorenzo stood, and wept: the forest tomb
Had marr'd his glossy hair which once could shoot
Lustre into the sun, and put cold doom
Upon his lips, and taken the soft lute
From his lorn voice, and past his loamed ears
Had made a miry channel for his tears.

XXXVI.

Strange sound it was, when the pale shadow spake;
For there was striving, in its piteous tongue,
To speak as when on earth it was awake,
And Isabella on its music hung:
Languor there was in it, and tremulous shake,
As in a palsied Druid's harp unstrung;
And through it moan'd a ghostly under-song,
Like hoarse night-gusts sepulchral briars among.

XXXVII.

然而在幽靈悲傷的眼中，

還閃爍著露水般晶亮的愛情，

這種光亮能夠驅逐恐懼的陰影，

讓可憐的女孩得到些許安詳，

傾聽幽靈講述那恐怖的時刻——

他訴說著傲慢和貪婪，還有狂妄的謀殺——

在隱蔽的松樹旁，在低窪處的水草邊，

他被祕密地殺害了。

XXXVIII.

幽靈還說，「伊薩貝拉啊，我的愛人！

我的頭上懸掛著紅色的越橘果，

我的腳下還壓著巨大的燧石；

周圍還灑落著柏樹

和高大栗樹的葉子和果實；

對岸綿羊的咩叫也響徹耳邊；

去吧，對著我頭上的野花撒一把清淚，

這樣會讓我在墳墓中得到莫大安慰。」

XXXVII.

Its eyes, though wild, were still all dewy bright
With love, and kept all phantom fear aloof
From the poor girl by magic of their light,
The while it did unthread the horrid woof
Of the late darken'd time, – he murderous spite
Of pride and avarice,—the dark pine roof
In the forest, – and the sodden turfed dell,
Where, without any word, from stabs he fell.

XXXVIII.

Saying moreover, "Isabel, my sweet!
"Red whortle-berries droop above my head,
"And a large flint-stone weighs upon my feet;
"Around me beeches and high chestnuts shed
"Their leaves and prickly nuts; a sheep—fold bleat
"Comes from beyond the river to my bed:
"Go, shed one tear upon my heather—bloom,
"And it shall comfort me within the tomb.

XXXIX.

「唉！唉！我現在只是個影子了，
我徘徊在人們居室的外面，
獨自唱著謝主的彌撒，
聽著在我身邊迴響的生命之音；
辛勤的蜜蜂在正午飛向田野，
無數教堂的鐘聲在報告著時間。
這些聲音讓我痛苦，熟悉而又陌生，
可是你卻留在了人間，離我遠遠的。」

XL.

「我對過去的一切都有感覺，
而我應該要發怒——若靈魂會發狂的話。
即使我已經失去了人間的幸福，
可幸福的餘味還在溫暖著我的墓穴，
就像從蒼穹中飛來一位天使做我的妻子，
你蒼白的臉色讓我覺得歡樂，
美麗日益增加，
我感覺有更崇高的愛情偷走了我的靈魂。」

XXXIX.

"I am a shadow now, alas! alas!

"Upon the skirts of human-nature dwelling

"Alone: I chant alone the holy mass,

"While little sounds of life are round me knelling,

"And glossy bees at noon do fieldward pass,

"And many a chapel bell the hour is telling,

"Paining me through: those sounds grow strange to me,

"And thou art distant in Humanity.

XL.

"I know what was, I feel full well what is,

"And I should rage, if spirits could go mad;

"Though I forget the taste of earthly bliss,

"That paleness warms my grave, as though I had

"A Seraph chosen from the bright abyss

"To be my spouse: thy paleness makes med;

"Thy beauty grows upon me, and I feel

"A greater love through all my essence steal."

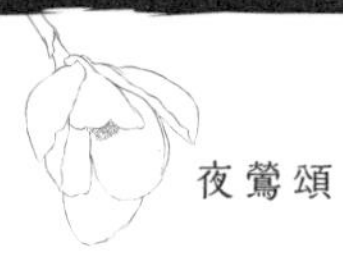

XLI.

幽靈呻吟著說，「再見了！」接著消逝無蹤，
只在黑暗中留下了輕微的騷動；
就像午夜中安然入睡的時候，
想到那些艱困時刻與徒勞無功，
我們會把頭埋入枕頭，
看到幽靈在黑夜中滾動和翻騰。
悲傷的伊薩貝拉感到眼皮疼痛，
天一亮，她就猛地坐起，睜開了眼睛。

XLII.

「哈哈！」她說，「誰能懂得這樣冷酷的人生？
我原本認為災難是最壞的事情，
原本以為命運只會讓人感到快樂和掙扎，
不是強烈的愉快，就是一命嗚呼；
沒想到還有哥哥血刃的罪惡！
親愛的幽靈，你讓我成熟了：
為此，我要去看看你，去吻你的眼睛，
朝朝暮暮，我向空中的你問好。」

XLI.

The Spirit mourn'd "Adieu!" – dissolv'd and left
The atom darkness in a slow turmoil;
As when of healthful midnight sleep bereft,
Thinking on rugged hours and fruitless toil,
We put our eyes into a pillowy cleft,
And see the spangly gloom froth up and boil:
It made sad Isabella's eyelids ache,
And in the dawn she started up awake;

XLII.

"Ha! ha!" said she, "I knew not this hard life,
"I thought the worst was simple misery;
"I thought some Fate with pleasure or with strife
"Portion'd us – happy days, or else to die;
"But there is crime – a brother's bloody knife!
"Sweet Spirit, thou hast school'd my infancy:
"I'll visit thee for this, and kiss thine eyes,
"And greet thee morn and even in the skies."

XLIII.

天已全亮，她做好打算
該如何偷偷地前往密林，
如果找到那塊珍貴的墳地；
就對著它唱一首安眠曲；
如何讓別人察覺不出她的暫別。
她要證實內心的夢境。
決定以後，她就帶了老保姆，
走進了陰森的樹林。

XLIV.

看啊，她們悄悄地沿著河邊走去，
她還不斷的對著老保姆低語著；
環顧四周之後，
她拿出了一把刀。──「我的孩子，你的內心
燃燒著怒火嗎？又有什麼好事，
能讓你重拾歡笑？」──暮色降臨，
他們找到了羅倫佐的所在：
巨大的燧石，懸掛著的越橘果。

XLIII.

When the full morning came, she had devised
How she might secret to the forest hie;
How she might find the clay, so dearly prized,
And sing to it one latest lullaby;
How her short absence might be unsurmised,
While she the inmost of the dream would try.
Resolv'd, she took with her an aged nurse,
And went into that dismal forest-hearse.

XLIV.

See, as they creep along the river side,
How she doth whisper to that aged Dame,
And, after looking round the champaign wide,
Shows her a knife. – "What feverous hectic flame
"Burns in thee, child? – What good can thee betide,
"That thou should'st smile again?" – The evening came,
And they had found Lorenzo's earthy bed;
The flint was there, the berries at his head.

XLV.

誰不曾在綠色的墓園中徘徊，

讓自己的靈魂像隻機警的鼴鼠，

鑽進黏黏的地層和堅硬的沙礫，

去窺探那棺中的頭顱、屍衣和枯骨？

誰都會痛惜那被死神玷污的身形，

想讓死者再恢復人類的靈魂，

啊！這種感覺再怎麼淒慘，

都比不上伊薩貝拉跪在羅倫佐的墓前！

XLVI.

她凝視著那一抔新土，

彷彿一眼就看透了它全部的祕密；

她看得很清楚，清楚得就像

在一口透明的井中看到白色的肢體；

她被謀殺現場所驚呆：

好像百合花在幽谷中掙扎，

突然，她拿起小刀向地下挖掘，

挖得比守財奴還要急切。

XLV.

Who hath not loiter'd in a green church-yard,
And let his spirit, like a demon-mole,
Work through the clayey soil and gravel hard,
To see skull, coffin'd bones, and funeral stole;
Pitying each form that hungry Death hath marr'd
And filling it once more with human soul?
Ah! this is holiday to what was felt
When Isabella by Lorenzo knelt.

XLVI.

She gaz'd into the fresh-thrown mould, as though
One glance did fully all its secrets tell;
Clearly she saw, as other eyes would know
Pale limbs at bottom of a crystal well;
Upon the murderous spot she seem'd to grow,
Like to a native lilly of the dell:
Then with her knife, all sudden, she began
To dig more fervently than misers can.

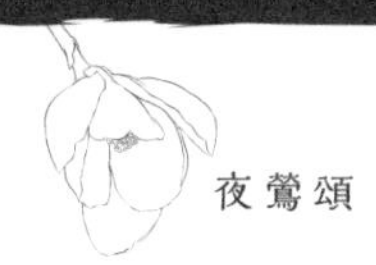

XLVII.

很快地，她挖出一隻髒手套，

手套上繡著她紫色的幻想，

她親吻著手套，但嘴唇比石頭還要冰冷，

又把手套貼在她的胸前，那手套結凍

寒冷刺骨，

那甘蜜能止住嬰兒的哭聲；

她又放手去挖掘，不作停留，

只時不時將長髮撩到腦後。

XLVIII.

老保姆在旁邊看著，心生疑問，

看著挖掘墳墓的淒涼景象，

內心也充滿了悲憐；

於是，她也披著一頭白髮跪下來，

用乾枯的雙手幫忙，

做著這恐怖的工作；她們挖掘了

三個小時，終於摸到了墓穴，

伊薩貝拉沒有頓足，也沒有叫嚷。

XLVII.

Soon she turn'd up a soiled glove, whereon
Her silk had play'd in purple phantasies,
She kiss'd it with a lip more chill than stone,
And put it in her bosom, where it dries
And freezes utterly unto the bone
Those dainties made to still an infant's cries:
Then 'gan she work again; nor stay'd her care,
But to throw back at times her veiling hair.

XLVIII.

That old nurse stood beside her wondering,
Until her heart felt pity to the core
At sight of such a dismal labouring,
And so she kneeled, with her locks all hoar,
And put her lean hands to the horrid thing:
Three hours they labour'd at this travail sore;
At last they felt the kernel of the grave,
And Isabella did not stamp and rave.

XLIX.

唉！為何總是描述這些恐怖陰森的狀況？
為何總是不斷講述著墓室之門？
古老的愛情故事應該是文雅的，
遊吟詩人的哀歌也是單純的！
親愛的讀者，還是請你讀讀
舊故事吧，因為我的詩篇實在
無法講得那麼好——最好閱讀原作，
傾聽那慘澹景象中貫穿的樂曲。

L.

她們的鋼刀比佩耳修斯的劍來得不鋒利，
她們割下的，不是畸形的妖魔的頭顱，
而是那位即使死後也如
生時那般儒雅的羅倫佐。古琴曾唱道：
愛情不會腐朽，她是主宰人類的神；
它也許是愛情的化身，死得過早，
伊薩貝拉正吻著它，輕聲啼哭。
這就是愛情——死了，卻不會廢黜。

XLIX.

Ah! wherefore all this wormy circumstance?
Why linger at the yawning tomb so long?
O for the gentleness of old Romance,
The simple plaining of a minstrel's song!
Fair reader, at the old tale take a glance,
For here, in truth, it doth not well belong
To speak: – O turn thee to the very tale,
And taste the music of that vision pale.

L.

With duller steel than the Persean sword
They cut away no formless monster's head,
But one, whose gentleness did well accord
With death, as life. The ancient harps have said,
Love never dies, but lives, immortal Lord:
If Love impersonate was ever dead,
Pale Isabella kiss'd it, and low moan'd.
'Twas love; cold, – dead indeed, but not dethroned.

LI.

她們急忙將頭顱偷帶回家，
它成了伊薩貝拉的寶貝：
她用金梳子梳理它淩亂的頭髮，
在雙眼陰森的凹陷處
整理每根睫毛；她用冰冷如石穴水滴般的
眼淚，將髒污的臉孔
洗滌乾淨——她邊梳邊嘆息，
整天不是親吻頭顱，就是哭泣。

LII.

後來她用一條絲巾——上面沾著
阿拉伯珍奇花卉的甜美露水，
還有各種彷彿從冰冷的花莖一湧而出
的奇異花汁——
她用絲巾包覆頭顱，又將花盆當作墳墓，
把它放在裡面，鋪上泥土，
種下一株羅勒花，
持續用淚水灌溉。

LI.

In anxious secrecy they took it home,

And then the prize was all for Isabel:

She calm'd its wild hair with a golden comb,

And all around each eye's sepulchral cell

Pointed each fringed lash; the smeared loam

With tears, as chilly as a dripping well,

She drench'd away: – and still she comb'd, and kept

Sighing all day—and still she kiss'd, and wept.

LII.

Then in a silken scarf,—sweet with the dews

Of precious flowers pluck'd in Araby,

And divine liquids come with odorous ooze

Through the cold serpent-pipe refreshfully, –

She wrapp'd it up; and for its tomb did choose

A garden-pot, wherein she laid it by,

And cover'd it with mould, and o'er it set

Sweet Basil, which her tears kept ever wet.

LIII.

從此，她忘了日月星晨，
從此，她忘了枝頭上蔚藍的天空，
忘了潺潺流水的山谷，
忘了寒冷的秋風；
她再也不知道白天何時逝去，
也不知朝陽何時升起，
只是靜靜地看著她的羅勒花，
並不斷用淚水灌溉它。

LIV.

由於她的淚水滋潤，
羅勒花長得茂盛，青翠欲滴；
佛羅倫斯所有的羅勒花都不及
它芬芳，因為它不但有淚水的澆灌，
還從人們懼怕的頭顱
得到所需的營養；
於是這寶貝就從密封的花盆裡
長出芬芳的嫩芽。

LIII.

And she forgot the stars, the moon, and sun,
And she forgot the blue above the trees,
And she forgot the dells where waters run,
And she forgot the chilly autumn breeze;
She had no knowledge when the day was done,
And the new morn she saw not: but in peace
Hung over her sweet Basil evermore,
And moisten'd it with tears unto the core.

LIV.

And so she ever fed it with thin tears,
Whence thick, and green, and beautiful it grew,
So that it smelt more balmy than its peers
Of Basil—tufts in Florence; for it drew
Nurture besides, and life, from human fears,
From the fast mouldering head there shut from view:
So that the jewel, safely casketed,
Came forth, and in perfumed leafits spread.

LV.

啊，憂鬱，在這兒稍停片刻吧！
啊，音樂，音樂，請黯然演奏吧！
還有回聲，回聲，對著我們嘆息吧，
未知的忘川，對著我們嘆息，喔，嘆息！
悲傷的精靈啊，抬頭微笑吧；
親愛的精靈啊，高舉你那沉重的頭，
讓幽暗的柏樹中射出光芒，
將你大理石的墓碑染上銀白的光。

LVI.

所有的悲傷都來這裡嗚咽吧，
請你們從悲劇女神的喉嚨出來，
從青銅的豎琴上鳴響淒慘的音樂，
輕彈琴弦，奏出神祕的哀歌；
請迎著輕風的悲哀低低吟唱吧，
因為，純真的伊薩貝拉不久
將離於人世：她日漸枯萎，如棕櫚樹，
被印度人砍伐，汁液流盡。

LV.

O Melancholy, linger here awhile!
O Music, Music, breathe despondingly!
O Echo, Echo, from some sombre isle,
Unknown, Lethean, sigh to us – O sigh!
Spirits in grief, lift up your heads, and smile;
Lift up your heads, sweet Spirits, heavily,
And make a pale light in your cypress glooms,
Tinting with silver wan your marble tombs.

LVI.

Moan hither, all ye syllables of woe,
From the deep throat of sad Melpomene!
Through bronzed lyre in tragic order go,
And touch the strings into a mystery;
Sound mournfully upon the winds and low;
For simple Isabel is soon to be
Among the dead: She withers, like a palm
Cut by an Indian for its juicy balm.

LVII.

啊，任由那株棕櫚樹獨自枯萎吧；
別讓寒冬在它臨終時刻降臨！
也許不會，但她那兩個拜金的
哥哥，看到了她死寂的雙眼
仍不斷地哭泣；很多好事的親友
覺得奇怪，為什麼她在即將成為
高貴新娘的時候，將青春和美貌
拋棄在一旁。

LVIII.

更使她的哥哥奇怪的是，
為什麼她總在羅勒花前垂頭坐著，
為什麼花兒像有魔力般盛開，
他們驚疑地猜測著事情的真相。
當然，他們沒想到
這微不足道的東西，竟能斷送
她美好的青春和歡愉，
甚至讓她不想念遲遲未歸的情人。

LVII.

O leave the palm to wither by itself;
Let not quick Winter chill its dying hour! –
It may not be – those Baalites of pelf,
Her brethren, noted the continual shower
From her dead eyes; and many a curious elf,
Among her kindred, wonder'd that such dower
Of youth and beauty should be thrown aside
By one mark'd out to be a Noble's bride.

LVIII.

And, furthermore, her brethren wonder'd much
Why she sat drooping by the Basil green,
And why it flourish'd, as by magic touch;
Greatly they wonder'd what the thing might mean:
They could not surely give belief, that such
A very nothing would have power to wean
Her from her own fair youth, and pleasures gay,
And even remembrance of her love's delay.

LIX.

所以，他們用心觀察，想探明
她的心事，卻久久徒勞無功；
因為她很少到教堂去懺悔，
也幾乎感受不到饑餓的煎熬；
她偶爾外出，也很快歸來，
像是鳥兒為了孵卵而匆匆回巢；
她也像雌鳥一樣耐心，靜靜地坐著
守著她的羅勒花，任淚珠沿著髮絲滾落。

LX.

他們還是偷走了羅勒花盆，
並暗地裡仔細考察：
花上染著青綠和死灰的痕跡，
那正是羅倫佐的臉：
啊，他們終於得到了謀殺的獎賞，
就匆忙間離開了佛羅倫斯，
永不回來。他們的頭上
流著罪惡的血跡，將他們流放異鄉。

LIX.

Therefore they watch'd a time when they might sift
This hidden whim; and long they watch'd in vain;
For seldom did she go to chapel-shrift,
And seldom felt she any hunger-pain;
And when she left, she hurried back, as swift
As bird on wing to breast its eggs again;
And, patient as a hen-bird, sat her there
Beside her Basil, weeping through her hair.

LX.

Yet they contriv'd to steal the Basil-pot,
And to examine it in secret place;
The thing was vile with green and livid spot,
And yet they knew it was Lorenzo's face:
The guerdon of their murder they had got,
And so left Florence in a moment's space,
Never to turn again. – Away they went,
With blood upon their heads, to banishment.

LXI.

唉，憂鬱，轉移你的目光吧！

哦，音樂，音樂，請黯然奏響吧！

哦，回聲，回聲，你改天再嘆息吧，

在忘川之島對我們嘆息吧！

悲傷的精靈啊，暫停你的喪歌吧，

因為伊薩貝拉，甜美的伊薩貝拉即將死去；

她死得孤寂，死得悲哀，

因為他們奪走了她的羅勒花盆。

LXII.

可憐的她看著死去與無感的物品，

熱切地追問她失去的羅勒花；

每當看到漫遊的朝聖者，她就用悅耳卻淒苦的聲音，

泣問著他為什麼把她的羅勒花

藏了起來，又藏在了哪裡；

為什麼不讓她見到；她哀訴著說：「誰這麼殘忍，

竟然偷走了我的羅勒花盆。」

LXI.

O Melancholy, turn thine eyes away!

O Music, Music, breathe despondingly!

O Echo, Echo, on some other day,

From isles Lethean, sigh to us—O sigh!

Spirits of grief, sing not your "Well—a—way!"

For Isabel, sweet Isabel, will die;

Will die a death too lone and incomplete,

Now they have ta'en away her Basil sweet.

LXII.

Piteous she look'd on dead and senseless things,

Asking for her lost Basil amorously;

And with melodious chuckle in the strings

Of her lorn voice, she oftentimes would cry

After the Pilgrim in his wanderings,

To ask him where her Basil was; and why

'Twas hid from her: "For cruel 'tis," said she,

"To steal my Basil-pot away from me."

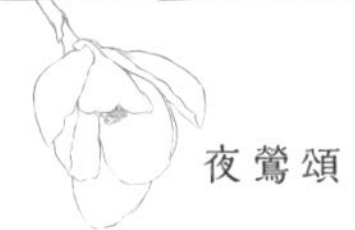

LXIII.

就這樣，她在憔悴孤寂中死去，

臨死之前，還一直追問著她的羅勒花盆，

佛羅倫斯的所有人都為她的愛情故事感到傷心，

對她表示憐憫，一起憂鬱。

有人將這悲涼的故事編成了

哀傷的歌曲，並且傳遍全城；

結尾是這樣唱的：「喔，太殘忍了！

是誰偷走了我的羅勒花盆！」

LXIII.

And so she pined, and so she died forlorn,

Imploring for her Basil to the last.

No heart was there in Florence but did mourn

In pity of her love, so overcast.

And a sad ditty of this story born

From mouth to mouth through all the country pass'd:

Still is the burthen sung – "O cruelty,

"To steal my Basil-pot away from me!"

關於作者

濟慈，全名約翰．濟慈（John Keats，1795—1821），出生於18世紀末年的倫敦，英國傑出的浪漫主義詩人。

約翰．濟慈出身卑微，他的父親是馬房飼養員。因父母早逝，他少年即成孤兒，生活貧困，在監護人的要求下習醫。但他自幼酷愛文學，1816年他認識了李．亨特和珀西．雪萊等作家，從此棄醫從文，專心於詩歌寫作。

1816年發表處女作《哦，孤獨》。1817年出版第一部詩集《詩歌》，收到了一些好評，但也有一些極為苛刻的攻擊性評論刊登在當時很有影響力的雜誌《Blackwood's magazine》上。濟慈沒有因此退縮，他在次年的春天付印了新詩集《恩底彌翁》（Endymion）。在接下來的幾年中，疾病與經濟上的問題一直困擾著濟慈，但他卻令人驚訝地寫出了大量優秀作品，其中包括《夜鶯頌》、《希臘古甕頌》、《秋頌》、《憂鬱頌》等名作，表現出詩人對大自然的強烈感受和熱愛，贏得了巨大聲譽，為英國和世界文學增添了光輝。

濟慈的一生是短暫的，1821年2月病逝，只活了26歲。在短暫的一生中，濟慈留下不少壯麗的詩篇。大詩人雪萊對濟慈的詩歌創作一向關心，經常和他通信。對於濟慈的早喪，雪萊深感悲痛，他為此寫了輓歌《阿童妮》，稱濟慈是「最活躍、最年輕的詩人」，「一棵露珠培育出來的鮮花」。

關於作品

哦，來喝一口美酒吧！喝一口
在地下深藏多年的清醇佳釀吧！
只消一口，就能令人想到花神和蔥籠的田野，
還有舞蹈、普羅旺斯的歌聲和似火的驕陽！

1819 年的春天，一隻夜鶯成了他們的鄰居，濟慈對夜鶯的歌聲非常喜愛。有一天，濟慈從餐桌旁搬了一把椅子，在葡萄樹下的草地上整整坐了一上午。後來，查理斯看到濟慈走到房間裡，將手裡的碎紙片塞到書架的角落裡——濟慈經常會將詩歌胡亂地寫在手邊的紙片上，之後要麼隨意地夾在書中，要麼就隨手扔掉——濟慈的這個壞習慣還是英國作家查理斯發現的。查理斯將碎紙片拿了出來，上面寫了一些關於夜鶯的文字。查理斯將它們復原，這就是那首膾炙人口的《夜鶯頌》。

濟慈的詩歌完美地體現了西方浪漫主義的特點，即用強調想像來突出文學的目的在於表現理想和希望；用強調自然來突出文學應偏重抒發個人的主觀感受和情緒；用強調象徵和神話來突出文學的隱喻性、表現性和誇張等藝術表現方式。詩人喜歡同時採用浪漫主義和現實主義的表現手法進行創作，既藝術地描寫美好的理想生活，又真實地再現當時的社會生活。才華橫溢的濟慈，與雪萊、拜倫齊名。雖然他英年早逝，但他留下來的詩篇卻帶給後人無限的精神享受。

約翰．濟慈生平年表

1795	0	10 月 31 日，出生於英國倫敦一間馬車行，為家中長子，有三個弟弟（其中之一在出生不久即夭折）與一個妹妹。
1802	7	到艾菲爾德學校就讀，開始接觸文學並嶄露頭角，翻譯、寫作方面常有獲獎，深受當時校長查爾斯．考登．克拉克（Charles Cowden Clarke）的欣賞，並與其子寇文．克拉克（Cowen Clarke）成為莫逆之交。
1804	9	父親意外從馬上跌落，傷重不治。從此家庭狀況一落千丈。
1810	15	母親因肺結核去世。商人理查．艾比（Richard Abbey）和約翰．羅蘭．桑德爾（John Rowland Sandell）成為濟慈的監護人。
		在艾比的要求下，濟慈離開艾菲爾德學校，進入一間倫敦醫院學習醫學。
1815	20	10 月，濟慈通過考試，順利成為蓋伊醫院的醫學生。但學醫之餘，濟慈對於文學仍保有渴望，這讓他對於未來是否從醫感到迷惘。
1816	21	濟慈毅然決然辭去實習外科醫生職位，全心投入文學。
		同年，寇文為他引薦當時名作家兼評論家李．亨特（Leigh Hunt），而後者也介紹珀西．比希．雪萊（Percy Bysshe Shelley）、威廉．華茲渥斯（William Wordsworth）等文人給他認識，將其帶入當時有影響力的文學圈內。

1817	22	在李・亨特的幫助下，濟慈出版第一本詩集。當時其作品雖有收到讚許，卻也在雜誌上遭受大量嚴苛的批評。 春天時，濟慈出版了《恩底彌翁（Endymion）》，是他以美麗的古希臘神話為背景所寫成的。全詩想像豐富，色彩絢麗，洋溢著對自由的渴望，但此作一出即飽受批評。 濟慈在外旅行時，接獲弟弟湯姆肺結核的消息，於是決定回到家鄉就近照顧弟弟。但不幸地，湯姆仍在年底逝世。
1818	23	濟慈在弟弟湯姆離開後便搬至漢普斯泰德（Hampstead）居住，在這裡遇見鄰居方妮・布朗（Fanny Brawne），並墜入愛河。但因為濟慈不穩定的經濟能力與健康狀況，兩人戀情不被女方家長認可，最終分開。
1819	24	雖然受到金錢與疾病的雙重壓力，濟慈仍在1819年寫出大量優秀且膾炙人口的作品。如《伊薩貝拉》、《聖艾格尼絲之夜》著名長詩，以及《夜鶯頌》、《秋頌》等篇都是在這一兩年完成。
1820	25	3月，約翰・濟慈開始出現肺結核症狀，身體逐漸衰弱，決定和方妮・布朗及故鄉朋友告別，前往義大利羅馬養病。
1821	26	2月23日，濟慈病逝於義大利羅馬，得年26歲。

濟慈詩選：夜鶯頌 /約翰濟慈著；王明鳳譯；
-- 初版. -- 臺北市：笛藤, 2022.04
面；　公分
中英對照
譯自：Ode to A Nightingale
ISBN 978-957-710-851-7（平裝）

873.51　　111004520

中・英對照雙語版

2022年4月28日　初版第1刷　定價300元

著　　者	約翰・濟慈
譯　　者	王明鳳
編　　輯	江品萱
美術編輯	王舒玗
總 編 輯	洪季楨
編輯企劃	笛藤出版
發 行 所	八方出版股份有限公司
發 行 人	林建仲
地　　址	台北市中山區長安東路二段171號3樓3室
電　　話	(02) 2777-3682
傳　　真	(02) 2777-3672
總 經 銷	聯合發行股份有限公司
地　　址	新北市新店區寶橋路235巷6弄6號2樓
電　　話	(02)2917-8022・(02)2917-8042
製 版 廠	造極彩色印刷製版股份有限公司
地　　址	新北市中和區中山路二段380巷7號1樓
電　　話	(02)2240-0333・(02)2248-3904
郵撥帳戶	八方出版股份有限公司
郵撥帳號	19809050

圖片來源：Unsplash